"Do I Fascinate You, Miss Glenn?"

Her quiet eyes were frankly appraising, and he lifted a dark eyebrow.

"Or are you looking for an appropriate place to plant a dagger?" he asked laughingly.

Amelia raised her chin. She wouldn't let this giant of a man intimidate her. "I was just thinking how amazing it is that the chair hasn't collapsed under your weight."

He laughed again, more softly, a laugh that sounded frankly predatory. "Were you? I'm not that big."

"No," she said with mock sincerity, "you're just a mountain of muscle, that's all."

His dark eyes narrowed as he studied her, and she wanted to back off and run. He disturbed her.

"I am not on the menu," she said boldly.

"Pity," he murmured. "You might taste better than you look."

Dear Reader,

Welcome to Silhouette! Our goal is to give you hours of unbeatable reading pleasure, and we hope you'll enjoy each month's six new Silhouette Desires. These sensual, provocative love stories are both believable and compelling—sometimes they're poignant, sometimes humorous, but always enjoyable.

Indulge yourself. Experience all the passion and excitement of falling in love along with our heroine as she meets the irresistible man of her dreams and together they overcome all obstacles in the path to a happy ending.

If this is your first Desire, I hope it'll be the first of many. If you're already a Silhouette Desire reader, thanks for your support! Look for some of your favorite authors in the coming months: Stephanie James, Diana Palmer, Dixie Browning, Ann Major and Doreen Owens Malek, to name just a few.

Happy reading!

Isabel Swift
Senior Editor

SDRL-7/85

DIANA PALMER
Love by Proxy

Silhouette Desire

Published by Silhouette Books New York

America's Publisher of Contemporary Romance

SILHOUETTE BOOKS
300 E. 42nd St., New York, N.Y. 10017

Copyright © 1985 by Diana Palmer

Distributed by Pocket Books

ISBN: 0-373-05252-9

First Silhouette Books printing December 1985

10 9 8 7 6 5 4 3 2 1

America's Publisher of Contemporary Romance

Printed in the U.S.A.

Books by Diana Palmer

Silhouette Romance

Darling Enemy #254
Roomful of Roses #301
Heart of Ice #314
Passion Flower #328
Soldier of Fortune #340

Silhouette Special Edition

Heather's Song #33
The Australian #239

Silhouette Desire

The Cowboy and the Lady #12
September Morning #26
Friends and Lovers #50
Fire and Ice #80
Snow Kisses #102
Diamond Girl #110
The Rawhide Man #157
Lady Love #175
Cattleman's Choice #193
The Tender Stranger #230
Love by Proxy #252

DIANA PALMER

is a prolific romance writer who got her start as a newspaper reporter. Accustomed to the daily deadlines of a journalist, she has no problem with writer's block. In fact, she averages a book every two months. Mother of a young son, Diana met and married her husband within one week: "It was just like something from one of my books."

One

Amelia Glenn tugged her beige trench coat closer around her body and tried not to giggle as she got off the elevator on the fourteenth floor of the Chicago office building. If only her fellow office workers at the agricultural equipment company could see her like this! The way that deathly dull job had been going lately, this was more a holiday than a favor for a friend.

She heard her bangles bunch at her wrists with a metallic ring and had to stand very still until they stopped, aware of curious stares from the two businessmen who'd come up with her on the elevator. Wouldn't they pass out if they knew what was under her coat!

She walked down the hall looking for office suite 1411, where she was due to deliver a special message. Ordinarily, Kerrie did this particular one, but she was out sick and Amanda had been recruited by her friend Marla Sayers to fill in. Marla's boyfriend was going to play a joke on his associate. It was only one message, after all, and Amelia did have the body for it, or so she was assured.

She was lean and tanned from head to toe, with a figure that could have modeled bikinis year-round. Her long, dark hair swung thickly as she walked, and her pale, dancing eyes were framed by black lashes, in a face whose features were as perfect as a cameo. She could have passed for a teenager.

There was, oddly, no one at the receptionist's desk when she walked in. Perhaps she was at lunch. Amelia laughed and started toward the office door. She gathered her nerve, because she'd never done this particular stunt before, pinned a smile to her full lips and breezed in.

Apparently there was a small conference going on. A big, very cold-looking man in a patterned shirt and no jacket was leaning over a graph of some kind on a huge oak desk. Around it were two shorter, paler men, hanging on every word. Amelia hadn't expected Wentworth Carson to be so big. He was as formidable as Marla's boyfriend had described him. All business, ice cold, nothing in him to attract a woman. Yes, she could have recognized him in a crowd. He wasn't handsome, not one bit. He had a big nose and bushy eyebrows and a pugnacious chin, and he looked more like a wrestler than an executive. He fit her nebulous image of a construction magnate all the way down to his big feet.

"Yes?" the big man asked coldly, looking up with eyes that were every bit as dark as the straight black hair that fell forward onto a broad forehead.

Amelia smiled wickedly. "Message for you, sir," she said. And she let the coat drop.

The two men grouped around the desk stared, gaping, with appreciative smiles and big eyes. The bigger man stood erect and looked angry.

Amelia had a passable voice—no threat to the Met, of course, put passable. She began to gyrate in her outlandish belly dancer's costume to the tune of the birthday song, inching slowly closer to the big, dark man.

He didn't look very receptive. In fact, he looked as if he'd like to pitch her out the window. That was even better. She laughed huskily as she went closer, her hips twitching, her skirts flying, her arms uplifted with the small cymbals on her fingers to show the high, soft curve of her breasts in their metallic casings.

"Happy birthday, honey," she added at the end, and just for pure spite, she went on tiptoe to kiss him full on his hard, chiseled mouth with as much enthusiasm as she could muster.

He kept his eyes open. His big body was rigid and he didn't move, not an eyelash, not a finger, not a breath. His mouth was hard and slightly cool, and totally unresponsive. He allowed the blatant caress for an instant, and then his huge, warm hands caught her bare waist and set her roughly on her feet. They released her immediately, as if he didn't like the feel of her taut, warm skin.

"What the hell kind of joke is this?" he asked coldly.

"It's a birthday greeting," she said, trying not to show how she really felt. Most people reacted in the spirit of fun that the messages intended, but it was a fact that this man wasn't going to appreciate the offbeat humor of his partner. She almost felt sorry for him. But she had to tell. It was part of the job.

"From whom?" he persisted, oblivious to the amused looks of his co-workers.

"Your partner, Andrew Dedham," she said.

"Then the joke is on him," he said coldly. "Because today is not my birthday."

She glared at him. "Then why didn't you say so at the beginning?" she challenged. "You surely didn't think I came in off the streets selling magazine subscriptions!"

His heavy brows lifted. "I wouldn't buy that kind of magazine," he said curtly.

Her eyes narrowed icily. "Why not, you look as if you could use some tutoring," she returned. "Frozen clean through, are we?" she added with a cold smile.

He seemed to grow three inches. "Whatever I am is none of your business. And if you aren't out that door in three minutes flat, I'll have you arrested for soliciting.''

"I am not a prostitute," she told him, sliding into her coat. "But if I were, honey, you wouldn't be rich enough!"

"I wouldn't be desperate enough," he corrected. "Out."

Just like that, as if she were a dog! She stared holes in him, but he only folded his arms over his formidable chest and glared back. Her eyes fell. She'd never encountered anybody like this giant dead fish, and she never wanted to again. From now on, Marla could do her own messages!

"When you do have your birthday, Mr. North Pole," Amelia said at the door, "I hope your birthday cake explodes in your face!"

"Just make sure you don't jump out of it," he returned coldly.

"I couldn't," she replied with a sweet smile. "The heat from all the candles would burn me alive!"

And she closed the door with a hard slam. Her hands trembled as she refastened the coat.

The receptionist came back in with a tray of Styrofoam cups obviously filled with coffee. She smiled in a friendly way. "Are you waiting to see Mr. Carson?" she asked. "Sorry I wasn't here, I just sneaked out to get them some coffee."

She remembered belatedly the name of this building. "The...Carson Building...wouldn't be...?" Amelia faltered.

"Yes, it would. Named for the late Angus. Did you want to see Mr. Carson?"

"I already have," Amanda said with a rueful laugh. "His poor wife."

The receptionist blinked. "Wife?"

Amelia was already at the other door, but she turned. "Isn't he married?"

"Not him," came the laughing reply. "There isn't a woman anywhere brave enough."

"I understand exactly what you mean. So long."

Two

Amelia was stoked up and fuming like a steam engine when she got back to Marla's office. She was dripping from the combined temperatures of Chicago in the summer and the winter trench coat she'd been wearing over the flamboyant belly dancer's costume.

Marla looked up, an elf with blond hair and blue eyes. "Well?" she asked, all wide smiles.

"Wentworth Carson," she began as she stripped off the trench coat and fumbled in Marla's office closet for her neat gray suit and blouse, "is a giant dead fish. He has the sense of humor of a giant dead fish, and he looks like a giant dead fish."

Marla, who'd known Amelia for almost a year, as long as the Georgia girl had been in Chicago, had never heard her fume before. She stared. "Andy said he had a sense of humor," she began.

"Where is it, visiting relatives in New York?" Amelia demanded.

Marla burst out laughing. She couldn't help it. "Oh, darling, I'm sorry, I know Andy didn't mean..."

"It wasn't his birthday," Amelia continued as she dragged on her slip and blouse and skirt with quick, methodical fury. "He said so. He accused me of being a prostitute. He threw me out of his office. He said not to jump out of his birthday cake. I hate him!"

Marla had long since buried her face in her hands on the desk, and her thin shoulders were shaking.

"What did you do?"

"I kissed him."

The laughter got worse.

"It made him furious, of course," Amelia said. She fumbled for a small brush in her purse and dragged it through the tangle of her hair. "I couldn't resist it, he looked so almighty arrogant. He should have tried to enjoy it, I can't imagine that he's ever been kissed by any woman who was actually willing and didn't have to be paid!"

Marla was just now catching her breath. "He did make an impression, didn't he?" she gasped. "I'm so sorry! If Kerrie hadn't been sick, you'd have been spared."

"I wouldn't go near that man again for anything," she grumbled. "He's a...a...a..."

"Giant dead fish?"

"Yes!"

"Andy will die when I tell him." Marla sighed. "I hope Wentworth Carson is a forgiving man, or my poor Andy will be out looking for work again."

"What possessed Andy to pull such a joke on a man like that?" Amelia asked. "He obviously has no sense of humor, and it wasn't even his birthday!"

"Maybe Andy didn't know that," Marla said comfortingly. She studied the older woman, dressed now in her familiar staid business clothes, her hair neatly arranged in a French twist. No one who saw her now would believe her capable of pulling off a joke like that.

"This is not how I want to spend my next hard-earned day off," Amelia said.

"Well, thanks a million for helping me out," Marla said and hugged the taller girl affectionately. "Andy will be thrilled, even if you aren't."

"I hope so. Tell him it was a sacrifice I'll never make again, will you?" She waved as she went out the door.

All the way home she thought about Wentworth Carson, and her teeth ground together. Horrible, humorless man, he must be the world's worst lover. He couldn't even kiss. Of course, he hadn't wanted to kiss her back. She flushed, remembering the hardness of his closed mouth. He seemed like a lonely man. She shook herself. *She* even felt sorry for squashed spiders, she reminded herself forcibly.

She went back to the sink in the small kitchen of the efficiency apartment she rented from a kindly couple in a residential area near the beach. It was really a garage apartment, but it had the advantage of being like a real house. She had the family, the Kennedys, nearby if she needed help, and she could walk to the beach. She had a phone of her own and even shared the family cat, Khan, a puffy Siamese-Persian, who visited her whenever she had chicken. She'd changed into a comfortable caftan and was just putting the finishing touches to tuna-salad sandwiches when her doorbell rang.

She frowned. Nobody ever came calling except Marla, and Marla went out with Andy practically every night now. It could be one of the Kennedys, of course, except that they were an elderly couple and never bothered her. Perhaps it was a salesman. She grinned, thinking up ways to get rid of him. Her social life was so dull that even a salesman became a welcome pest. It was great fun deciding how to get rid of them tactfully.

The last one had been selling subscriptions to an underwater publication. She promised to send a check as soon as her sunken living-room pool was finished. She'd closed the door on a face like a mask as he tried to decide between going meekly away or calling the nearest sanitarium on her behalf.

She opened the door as far as the chain latch would allow—it was night, after all—and came face to face with the enemy.

Her pale blue eyes glared at him through the crack. "I do not give private performances," she informed Wentworth Carson.

"Thank God," he returned. "Are you going to open the door, or would you like it removed?"

Heavens, he was the size of a battering ram! The Kennedys would surely throw her out if he put his shoulder to it....

With an angry sigh, she opened the door and let him in. He was wearing a trendy blue blazer with an unbuttoned white shirt and white slacks, and a dark pelt of hair showed in the opening at his olive tan throat. He looked different than he had that afternoon in his office. Big and broad and oddly sensuous for a cold fish. He made her nervous.

He stared down at her with a frown, his eyes on the blue-green-and-gold striped caftan she was wearing, with bare feet, no makeup and her dark hair still in its neat French twist.

"Are you Amelia Glenn?" he asked as if he couldn't quite believe it.

"Surely you don't make mistakes, Mr. Carson?" she asked with a false smile. "I'd never believe it!"

"You look more mature," he said.

She glared at him. "You mean I look older. I was twenty-eight last month, in fact," she said. "About half your age...?" she added pointedly.

"I'm forty," he replied.

"Twelve years your junior," she corrected smugly. "I do feel a mere child by comparison."

He scowled blackly. She wondered if he ever smiled. He put his hands into his slacks pockets and stared at her openly.

"Miss Sayers tells me you don't work for her."

"No, I don't." She turned back toward the kitchen. "You're welcome to join me if you like tuna fish," she said over her shoulder.

He closed the door and followed her into the kitchen, pulling out a chair at the small table. "Is this called Southern hospitality, or do I look under-fed?"

She couldn't help the laughter. "Underfed, my foot. I'd hate to have your grocery bill."

"I have to watch what I eat," he said frankly. "Even then, I work out at the gym to keep from looking like a walking beer barrel."

She laughed again, and reddened. "Sorry."

"No offense taken. What do you do for a living?"

She poured coffee into two handmade pottery cups, her eyebrows asking if he drank coffee, and he nodded.

"I'm a clerk typist for an agricultural equipment firm," she said.

His eyebrows arched.

"Well, I am," she grumbled. "What do I look like?"

He actually smiled. Or it could be a muscle spasm, she thought wickedly. "I expected a more exotic oc-cupation," he returned.

"I grew up working in a print shop. The most exotic thing I've ever done in my life I did this afternoon, to help Marla out."

"Andy Dedham started working for me last month," he said as she sat down and shoved a platter of sandwiches between them on the table. "He doesn't know me very well yet, but he'll learn. I am going to pay him back in kind, and you're going to help me. In costume, of course."

She froze. "How?"

"His mother," he replied, toying with his cup of black coffee, "is from Boston. She is a saintly widowed lady with impeccable manners, and once a month she comes to town and takes him to La Pierre for an elegant dinner."

"Oh, no." She shook her head. "Oh, no, I couldn't, not there! All those people…! And Marla would never forgive me!"

"Where's your spirit of adventure, Miss Glenn?"

"Under the table, hiding," she returned. "I can't! Furthermore," she added with hauteur, "I won't!"

He considered that, watching her with pursed lips. "Suppose I had a male stripper appear for you, at your sainted place of work?" he asked pleasantly.

She went violently red, gaping at him. "Oh, no, you couldn't. Mr. Callahan would fire me on the spot!"

He smiled, very slowly. "Would he, really?"

"You wouldn't!"

"Get in your rig, Cleopatra, be at La Pierre tomorrow night at exactly 7:00 P.M. and ask for Carlos when you get to the door," he said. "Everything will be arranged. If not," he added, studying her carelessly, "the morning after, you will have a particularly nauseating visitor, G string and all."

She buried her face in her hands. "I'd die!"

"My, my, aren't you a paradox?" he murmured on a deep chuckle. "You seemed to enjoy your role enough, when the shoe was on the other foot."

"I didn't embarrass you," she countered. "That can't be done!"

"That's true enough," he affirmed. He leaned back in his chair, all blatant masculinity, big and dark and frankly sexy, with that shirt unbuttoned just enough to make her wonder what was under it. Dark hair peeked out of the opening, and a deeply tanned throat. He was as sensuous as any man she'd ever encountered, and twice the size of most of her dates. She would have found him fascinating under other circumstances.

Her quiet eyes were frankly appraising, and he lifted a dark eyebrow.

"Do I fascinate you, Miss Glenn?" he asked on a laugh. "Or are you looking for an appropriate place to plant a dagger?"

She raised her chin to show him she wasn't intimidated. "I was just thinking how amazing it is that the chair hasn't collapsed under your weight."

He laughed softly, laughter that had a frankly predatory sound. "Were you? I'm not that big."

"No," she said with mock sincerity, "you're just a small mountain, that's all."

His dark eyes narrowed as they appraised her, and she wanted to back off and run. He disturbed her.

"I am not on the menu," she said boldly.

"Pity," he murmured. "You might taste better than you look."

She lifted her cup and cocked her head to one side.

"I wouldn't," he said calmly. "You'd have to spend the evening washing up."

She sighed angrily. "I don't like you."

He smiled slowly. "If I hadn't learned so much about your sex the hard way, I might be tempted to make you like me," he said very quietly. "But fortunately for you, I've lost my taste for it. An occasional night out satisfies me very well these days."

He sounded and looked as if women held no more secrets for him, and she felt vaguely grateful that he wasn't interested in her. A man like that, with his obvious experience, could make mincemeat of her.

"Excuse me while I get down on my knees and give thanks for that saving grace," she told him and offered him the sandwiches.

He took one and studied it carefully.

"Looking for something?" she asked as she lifted one for herself.

"Arsenic," he said bluntly.

She burst out laughing. "I used the last on the bus driver who let me off a mile from my stop," she promised. "Honestly, it's safe."

He bit into it, finished it and smiled. "Not bad. I didn't know tuna could taste so good."

"It's the pickled peach juice," she murmured dryly. "Dad taught me how to make it. He does most of the cooking. My mother can burn water."

"What does she do?"

"She sets type for my father, who runs the print shop. She's very good at that, and dealing with customers, but she isn't domestic. I learned to cook or starve at an early age." She finished her own sandwich and took a sip of coffee. "How long have you been in construction?" she asked politely.

His broad shoulders shrugged as he finished his second sandwich. "I think I was born doing it. My parents died when I was just a child. My grandmother raised me, pushed me into finding a profession I liked instead of just one I took for money." He smiled faintly. "I found I enjoyed building things. She prodded me until I called up a cousin who was an architect and asked him point-blank how I could get into the business. He was impressed enough to hire me on the spot. I worked for him between college classes. When I graduated he gave me an executive position." His eyes grew wistful. "He had no immediate family, and he hated most of his distant relatives. When he died, I inherited the company. I've expanded it, enlarged it. Now it's almost too big for me. I have a board of directors and every damned decision I make, I have to fight for."

"I'm glad I'm just a tadpole," she said with a sigh. "I'd hate that."

"I enjoy it," he murmured, dark eyes smiling at her across the table. "I like the challenge. It keeps my blood pumping."

At his age, surely a family would help. She studied him for a long moment, unaware of the blatant curiosity in her eyes.

"Well?" he asked. "Spit it out."

She shifted in the chair, feeling her nudity under the caftan as if he'd reached out and touched her. She hadn't been self-conscious with him before, but now she wished she was dressed.

"I just wondered why you weren't married."

"Because I don't want to be," he replied. His dark eyes sparkled mischievously. "Or did you think I was over the hill? I assure you, I'm not. At least, not in the respect you're mulling over," he added, watching her fidget nervously. He finished his coffee. "Are you going to La Pierre, or do I make a phone call?" he asked.

She sighed defeatedly. "I'll go. But I'll never forgive you."

"That won't matter," he said. "We won't see each other again." He stood up. "Thanks for the meal."

"You're welcome."

She walked him to the door, expecting him to go right out it. But he didn't. He turned and suddenly put his big hands on either side of her face and tilted it up to his dark eyes.

"Just to set you right on something..." he murmured, and bent his head.

His mouth came down on hers roughly, a warm assault that quickly parted her set lips and searched them with a pressure that was demanding and frankly expert. Within seconds, she was his, a victim turned co-conspirator, a willing victim with a frantic heartbeat. She'd been kissed before, infrequently, but it had never been like this. She wanted it to go on forever. Her eyes were closed, her fists clenched tightly by her sides, her body throbbing even though he didn't touch it or bring her one inch closer. She savored the rough pressure of his lips on hers and tasted him in one wild second with all the sensual curiosity she'd ever experienced for a man.

His head lifted a fraction of an inch and he looked into her drowsy, dazed eyes. "Why, you little fraud," he breathed. "It was pure bravado this morning, wasn't it? You don't even know how!"

She almost said "teach me," she almost reached up to him. But sanity came back just in the nick of time. She eased away from him, her eyes nervous but steady on his face.

"Are you through?" she asked through lips swollen from the pressure of his mouth, which had, at the last, been formidable.

"Yes." He studied her with a ghost of a smile on his broad, craggy face. "Odd how things happen. I'm sorry we come from such different walks of life. I'd have enjoyed teaching you. A twenty-eight year old innocent," he added with a visible twinkle in his dark eyes, "is an intriguing proposition."

"You just take your propositions and go away and play with your building blocks. I'll do your dirty work. And you keep that male stripper away from my office, please, I need my job."

"Seven sharp," he returned. He opened the door with a last, lingering look. "You could make your living as an exotic dancer," he said quietly. "I've never seen a more exquisite body."

He turned and left her standing there. It was a full minute before she could close the door again. Cold fish, indeed! More like a dormant volcano....

Three

———

Mr. Callahan was around sixty, had a bald head and narrow little eyes, wore glasses and was half Amelia's size. He could outcurse any sailor in port on a spree, and his compassion stopped at the door of his plant. He did not give leaves of absence, he did not like illness, and if there had been another job going anywhere, Amelia would have taken it on the spot. But openings were so hard to find in the raw economic times that she gritted her teeth and did what she was told. The only thing worse than this would be going back to Seagrove, a small town on the coast near Savannah, Georgia, and helping her parents run the print shop. That would take her close to Henry Janrett, who still expected her to come home and marry him when she got big-city living out of her blood. Henry ran the small town's sole newspaper. He wrote a column about beekeeping, when he wasn't lazing around local officials' offices jotting down notes. He was a sweet man, just about Amelia's own age, and she supposed someday she might even give in and do it. But Henry seemed a desperate last chance, and meanwhile she was still hoping for a crack at an exciting occupation in the big city. She didn't know why she'd picked Chicago. Perhaps because her Navy veteran mother had been stationed at a naval base near Chicago during World War II and had come to Chicago on leave, and Amelia had heard such fascinating things about the Windy City. Perhaps it was its ancient gangster history. She'd come here a year ago in a last-ditch attempt to find something her life lacked, before she went over the hill completely. She'd been hoping for excitement and adventure. And she'd found Mr. Callahan.

She groaned as she filled out another order form. Then she thought about what she had to do at 7:00 P.M. and groaned again. She called Marla at lunch and asked if she could borrow the belly dancer's costume.

"Why?" Marla asked.

"I don't have time for deep questions," Amelia grumbled. "Can I or can't I?"

"Well...sure. He went to see you, didn't he? I had to give him your address, you just can't say no to him; but I thought he was going to mail you a letter...."

"I can't tell you what it's all about, so don't ask."
Amelia sighed. "But Andy isn't going to like it."

"What is he having you do? Oh, Amelia, you can
tell me, I'm your friend!"

Mr. Callahan came out of his office, saw her on the
phone and glared.

"Yes, sir," Amelia said calmly, "that's right, our
new manure spreader can handle all your require-
ments."

"What?" Marla faltered.

"If you'll get your order right in the mail.... Oh,
you're just checking on it, you don't want to place an
order at this time? But you are keeping us in mind?
How nice of you, sir!"

Marla was giggling. "Mr. Callahan, I presume? See
you later, darling."

"Yes, sir, certainly. Goodbye." Amelia hung up and
gave Mr. Callahan a bright smile.

He nodded approvingly. "Nice public relations
work, girl. Very nice." He walked on by, and Amelia
tried not to slide down in her chair with relief.

Of course, Marla was waiting like a big spider when
Amelia got to her office late that evening.

"What are you going to do, and where?" Marla
asked. "You've got to tell me! What has that man put
you up to?"

"I can't tell you," Amelia groaned, knowing that
Marla would rush to tell Andy, and then she'd have a
male stripper in her office...arrrgh!

"I'm your friend," Marla coaxed.

"So far, so good, will you swear out an affidavit to that effect and keep it on hand, I may need it," she murmured as she drew on the belly dancer's costume and tugged her trench coat over it. "This is getting to be a real drag, you know?" she muttered.

"Where are you going?" Marla asked.

"Out to eat."

"Where?"

The phone rang in time to save her. Marla answered it, and Amelia got her purse and started out the door.

"Yes, of course I understand, I'll see you tomorrow," Marla was saying. "Yes, I'm sure the weather's cooler there. It's too bad she's sick."

Amelia waved and left. Rather than walk, she got a cab across town to the French restaurant. She walked in, nervous, fuming, and asked for Carlos.

The hostess gave her a blank stare. "I beg your pardon?"

"I want to speak to Carlos," Amelia said again. "He's expecting me."

"To do what?" the hostess burst out, staring at the trench coat, which showed no blouse or skirt or slacks.

Amelia leaned forward. "I'm stark naked," she said with a stage leer. "I'm supposed to jump out and scare an old lady in there. Now will you please get Carlos?"

"Yes, ma'am!" the hostess said quickly, backing away.

Amelia blew a wisp of hair out of her eyes. Of all the hangups, why did it have to happen to her? She glared around her, hating the elegant restaurant, hating Wentworth Carson, hating the whole world. Things had been going so well lately....

It seemed to take forever to get Carlos. But minutes later she heard footsteps and turned to see a tall, very somber policeman walking toward her.

"Okay, lady," the policeman said, and brought out a pair of handcuffs. "Let's go see the sergeant."

"No!" Amelia burst out. "No, you can't! I'm here for a legitimate reason. Let me show you!"

She started to unbutton the trench coat, and the policeman quickly got her hands behind her and whipped on the handcuffs.

"No, you don't!" the policeman said quickly. "No flashing! Honest to God, you college kids give me a pain. Thanks for calling me, Dolores. I'll take care of her. Come on, honey."

"Thanks, Dolores," Amelia sputtered at the stunned hostess. "I'll do you a favor someday. What're your favorite colors, and I'll send flowers along with the bomb."

"Terrorist threats and acts," the policeman muttered as he led her toward the waiting squad car. "Honest to God, you could get ten years."

Amelia started to speak just as a photographer rushed up and exploded a flashbulb in her face.

"Open the coat, honey, open the coat, let's get some good pics!" the photographer called, and the policeman put her in the car and went forward to argue with the photographer.

Amelia sank back against the seat and closed her eyes. *There are days,* she thought pleasantly, *when it's just the very devil to get out of bed at all.*

She eventually got everything straightened out. But it took a phone call to a very upset Marla, who had to come downtown and explain everything to the desk sergeant, who looked like a man who'd heard everything once and didn't have a spare nerve left in his entire body.

"I will die, I will just die," Amelia moaned when she and Marla were back at the Kennedys' garage apartment. "Imagine me being arrested! Arrested! And for flashing.... I will kill that man," she said, wide-eyed. "I will kill him stone-cold dead."

"I may help you," Marla said darkly. "Imagine, setting up poor Andy and his mother that way." She frowned. "But, darling, Andy had gone home to see about his mother. She got sick early this morning."

Amelia stopped and blinked. "What?"

"Andy went home."

"But he told me to go to La Pierre tonight," she gasped. "He told me to ask for Carlos...." She moaned again. "And there was a photographer! He took my picture!"

Marla stared at her. "What if he was a press photographer?"

She buried her head in her hands. "I'll die."

"Well, maybe he wasn't. You get a good night's sleep, and in the morning it will all seem like a bad dream, you'll see." Marla hugged her. "You've had an awful night, I know. Just have a nice bath and go to sleep, and in the morning it will be all right."

"Will it?" Amelia asked pitifully, needing reassurance.

"Really."

But in the morning, she went to get her newspaper. And when she opened it, there she was, shocked face and all, on the front page, being arrested in a trench coat. And the cutline read, "Who says flashing is passé? This young lady was arrested au naturel at Chez Pierre last night for attempting to flash the exclusive clientele. Tough luck, isn't she lovely?"

She closed the newspaper just as the phone rang. She didn't need even one guess.

"Hello, Mr. Callahan," she said hopefully.

"You're fired!" he yelled, and hung up.

She sat down with a sigh beside her cooling morning coffee. So much for things getting better.

After she dressed, she phoned Marla. "I want Mr. Wentworth Carson's address."

"Darling..." Marla began.

"You call Andy and find out for me where he lives. I am not going to do this at his office, I am going to go to his home and kill him where he stands."

"But, darling...."

"Do it." She hung up.

Several harrowing hours later, after she'd exhausted the terrifying possibilities of unemployment and the rent being due, she drove up the long, winding driveway of an estate in Lincoln Park. It was an exclusive neighborhood, and she wasn't shocked by the very elegant and enormous brick home sitting at the end of that flowery, tree-shaded drive. She parked her elderly but respectable Ford at the front door and got out, glaring at the white Rolls Royce as she passed by on her way up the steps.

She was wearing her gray business suit with a sedate white blouse and white accessories. She looked very prim and proper with her hair in a bun and the minimum of makeup. And she only wished she could drive a tank into the front door. She wanted to make a very good impression on Wentworth Carson. A lasting, physical impression.

She rang the bell. An elderly man opened the door and smiled at her. "Yes, madam, may I help you?"

"I am here to see Wentworth Carson," she said quietly.

"Mr. Carson is in the study," he said. "May I announce you?"

"You may not," she replied, pushing past him. "I will announce myself. Which way is the study, please?"

The elderly man hesitated, but his restraint was unnecessary. Wentworth Carson himself was standing in the doorway of the plushly carpeted room, wearing slacks and a burgundy knit shirt, hands in slacks pockets, staring at her.

"Miss Glenn," he said politely.

"Mr. Carson," she replied with equal politeness.

"Why are you here?" he asked curtly. "And how did you get this address?"

"Those questions are hardly relevant." She produced a folded newspaper from under her arm and handed it to him.

He frowned and then opened the paper. His eyes blinked as he read. His head lifted. "What the hell did you do, woman?"

"I went to La Pierre to surprise Andy."

He was trying not to laugh. "Well, it was all for nothing, wasn't it? He didn't show up." He glanced at her. "But didn't you look at the sign?"

Her head moved a little. "What?"

"Didn't you look at the sign?"

He handed her the paper. She looked. There on the marquis was "Chez Pierre."

She felt faint. But she was made of sturdy stuff. During the Civil War one of her great-grandmothers had held off a company of Yankees for two days until help arrived to vanquish them. Amelia stood erect.

"Andy was at home with his mother," she said.

"Yes, I know. I hadn't expected him to come into the office, and he didn't call me until last night. I didn't have time to warn you."

She was still staring blankly at him. "I got arrested. They took me to jail. They booked me. I was fingerprinted. They thought I was naked. I told them I wasn't, but they wouldn't listen. They locked me up!'' Her eyes got wilder as she went along. ''My father subscribes to this paper.'' She held it up. ''He likes to know what's going on in the city where his daughter lives.'' She stared down at the newspaper. ''What a shock this will be. I've never even worn shorts downtown back home.''

He couldn't help it. He laughed. That only made it worse. She flung the paper on the floor while the elderly butler tried diligently to keep a straight face.

''Mr. Callahan called me this morning. He fired me. Now I'll have to go back home. The people in the post office will see that paper, and so will the mail carrier, and the mail carrier will tell his wife, and she'll tell the ladies at church....'' Her lower lip trembled as tears threatened. ''I hate you. And I made Marla get your address from Andy so that I could come here and tell you how much I hate you. I hope your Rolls Royce rusts!''

She turned around and started out the door, just as a quavering voice asked, ''Who is that, Worth?''

The voice was of someone the butler's age, but feminine. Through tears, Amelia saw a tiny old woman moving into the hall from the room on the other side of the house. She could hardly walk; her gnarled hands were on a padded walker. She stood just inside the hall and looked for all the world like a cuddly toy. She smiled, brightening her blue eyes and her pale, wrinkled complexion.

"Hello," she said softly.

"H-hello," Amelia said, and even managed a watery smile.

"I couldn't help hearing," the older woman apologized. "Worth hardly ever guffaws like that; it woke me from my nap. Are you the young lady he was bellowing about last night? You don't look like a belly dancer."

"Actually, I'm a retired ax murderer," Amelia said with a cold glare at Wentworth Carson. "Just recently retired."

"Thank goodness, I'm sure I wouldn't enjoy being murdered. Do you drink tea, my dear?"

"Grandmother, I'm sure Miss Glenn has packing to do," the big man said, as if the prospect of having her out of the city delighted him.

Amelia glared at him. "I like tea."

"Then do come and have a cup with me," the old woman said. "I'm Jeanette Carson. Worth is my grandson."

"How lovely for you," Amelia said. She gave Worth a glance and followed the little old lady into the elegance of rosewood and silk furniture and immaculate white carpeting. "My name is Amelia Glenn."

"I'm very pleased to meet you, my dear. I adore white, as you see. Impractical, but so lovely," Jeanette Carson said. She eased down on the sofa in front of a long, polished coffee table, and rang a bell. A young woman in uniform appeared and was told to bring tea.

"That was Carolyn," Jeanette said. "Worth hasn't run her off yet, but I do believe he's giving it his best. He prefers to have me surrounded with men here. He's sure I can get around women, but he believes that men can handle me. Ha!" She laughed. Her wrinkled face drew up indignantly. She sighed. "Anyway, he never brings young ladies home these days. I was simply shocked when he mentioned you. I didn't know about you, you see."

"Oh, Worth and I are great friends," she said, smiling poisonously at the big man who joined them. "Aren't we?"

He stared at her. "You and I, friends? God forbid!"

"Don't you worry, we will be. You'll get used to me, you lucky man," she added with a cold smile.

"You brought your troubles on yourself, Miss Glenn," he said. He sat down, hitching up his pants. "You should take some spelling courses."

She glared at him. "If it hadn't been for you, I wouldn't have gone to the restaurant in the first place."

"You started it," he reminded her. He leaned back in his chair and smiled at her challengingly.

"I do seem to have missed something," Jeanette broke in, glancing from one to the other.

"Lucky you." Amelia smiled.

"Miss Glenn was arrested in the early hours for—" he paused for effect "—flashing, wasn't it?"

She glared at him. "I was arrested for wearing a belly dancing costume under a trench coat," she told the elderly woman, "at Wentworth's instructions."

Jeanette gasped as she stared at her grandson. "You sent this young woman to an elegant French restaurant in a belly dancing costume?"

His dark eyes narrowed at Amelia. "She came waltzing into my office wearing it, sang me a birthday song and kissed me."

Jeanette leaned forward. "Don't be ridiculous, Worth, it isn't your birthday."

"I know that!" he burst out. "It was a practical joke one of my employees played on me. Almost," he added darkly, "an ex-employee."

"Now, now, Wentworth, you wouldn't really fire him?" Amelia taunted.

"Worth," he said irritably. "No one calls me Wentworth."

"I can think up some better names," Amelia said sweetly. "Perhaps you'd like to hear them, at length, some other time?"

"That isn't likely," he said firmly. "You'll be out of town."

"Out of town?" Jeanette frowned. "Why?"

"She lost her job," Wentworth Carson said.

"Then, dear, you must give her another one," Jeanette said. "It's the least you can do, since it's your fault she lost it."

"It is not my fault," he said. "And I don't have a job to give her," he added smugly, "there are no vacancies."

"In that case, she can work for me," Jeanette said haughtily. "I need a social secretary. Someone to fetch and carry and help me get around town. God knows, you're never here in the daytime."

Worth sat up straight, as if he didn't believe what he was hearing. "Social secretary?"

"Yes," Jeanette said. She gave him a dogged glare, and the resemblance between the two of them was so noticeable that Amelia almost smiled.

He glared at Amelia.

"I didn't come here looking for a job," she said in all honesty to Jeanette. "I only came to kill your grandson."

"Too messy on white carpet," Jeanette said, shrugging it off and smiling as Carolyn brought in the big silver tea service. "Work for me instead. You can even live in, if you like."

"Hell, no," Worth said quietly.

"Wentworth!" Jeanette chided.

He got up and walked out of the room, muttering things under his breath as he slammed the door behind him.

"Now that he's out of the way, let's talk business," Jeanette said, smiling at her guest. "I'm seventy-five, I have a temper as bad as my grandson's, I'm overbearing and pushy and I never ask when I can demand." She sat back, tea in hand. "I'm recovering from a broken hip and it's hard for me to get around. Worth practically keeps me in chains. And I want to break out. You can help me."

"You don't know me," Amelia began.

Jeanette stared at her. "In my day," she said, "I was one of the best investigative reporters in Chicago. I am a dandy judge of character even to this day. I may not know you now, but I will. And so far, you pass with flying colors. Now," she said. She named a figure twice what Callahan had paid Amelia. "Does that suit you? And would you like to live in?"

"I would, if only to spite your grandson, but I signed a one-year lease where I am, and I like my landlords very much," she confessed. "Besides," she added, "I like my privacy. There simply isn't any when you live with other people."

"How old are you, dear?"

"Twenty-eight."

"Parents?"

"Both living. They have a print shop back home in Georgia."

Jeanette stared into her tea. "And is there a man in your life?"

She sighed. "Not unless you count Henry. He runs the paper back home and would marry me on a sunny day if it weren't too inconvenient and didn't happen on press day."

Jeanette laughed softly. "We're going to get along very well. Yes, we are."

Amelia thought so, too. But when she came out two hours later, Wentworth Carson was waiting outside in the yard, hands in pockets and glaring holes in her.

"What a snit we're in," Amelia chided. "Talk about bad-tempered people..."

"It is not my fault you lost your job," he told her bluntly. "And I like my life as it is. I want no part of you here. Tell my grandmother you won't take the job."

"I like your grandmother," she said curtly. "She's just like my mother, crusty and unflappable and impossible to fool. I'll take care of her."

He stared harder. "In return for what?" he asked, narrowed eyes telling her everything he wasn't saying.

"How often is she taken advantage of?" she asked instead.

"Her heart is as big as the world," he said. "She likes strays."

"I am not a stray. I have owners."

"Go home."

"I can't."

"Why?"

"Because I'd have to marry Henry!" she burst out. "If he'd still have me after he saw a copy of this morning's paper. My reputation will be in shreds."

"Why not marry Henry?" He frowned.

"Because the most exciting thing he ever said to me was, 'Amy, your nose has a crook in it.'"

His eyebrows lifted. "Not a passionate man."

"No."

His dark eyes roamed over her neat suit. "Are you a passionate woman?"

"That's something you'll never need to know. I am going to work for your grandmother, not get involved with you," she told him firmly.

One corner of his disciplined mouth turned up. "She likes you. She'll spend her days throwing you at my head and her nights finding more ways to get us married."

"You're safe," she told him, turning toward her old Ford. "I don't like older men."

"Forty is not old," he said shortly.

"At twenty-eight, it is old," she returned, facing him squarely. "I want somebody to play with."

He started laughing, and only then did she realize how he'd interpreted what she said. Her face flamed.

"Baseball!" she burst out. "Tennis and swimming and jogging, not...not...*that*!"

He laughed harder. She didn't say another word. She crawled into her car and managed with the greatest of difficulty to get it turned around and headed out of the yard. He was still standing there laughing when she drove away.

Four

Amelia showed up for work the next morning at eight-thirty sharp, wearing a sedate gray ensemble that made her pale blue eyes look slate-gray to match it. The skirt and knit blouse were worn with a trendy little short-sleeved cotton jacket, and she put her hair in a neat bun. She wasn't giving Wentworth Carson any cause for complaint with the way she dressed.

When she pulled up in front of the house, a short, elderly yardman motioned her to move the car down to the garage. She cranked the engine again, with difficulty. The old yellow Ford had a habit of refusing to turn on again after the engine got hot. It was one of those ghostly problems that several mechanics hadn't been able to solve, so she lived with it. But today it did crank, eventually, and she pulled it with a clank and a clatter down to the elegant, spacious garage where Wentworth's Rolls and a Mercedes were parked.

It made her feel odd, parking between two such luxurious vehicles, and she was half afraid that she might accidentally scratch one of them. But it was obvious that Wentworth didn't want her pitiful old wreck parked in front of his house. And that irritated her no end. Snob, she thought angrily.

She'd worked herself into a fever of resentment by the time she got to the front door. Well, he needn't think she was going to skulk up the back stairs like a servant. She was as good as he was, any day!

The maid opened the door for her with a smile. "Come in, please. Mrs. Carson is still asleep, but Mr. Worth said you're to have breakfast with him in the dining room. Follow me, please."

Breakfast with Worth, she thought, how lucky could a working girl get?

He was sitting at the head of the table with a cup of coffee and a pile of toast at his elbow. He glanced up when she came into the room, his eyes dark and steady and expressionless.

"What a treat," he taunted. "Breakfast with the terror of the Egyptian tombs."

"I am not a mummy," she countered. "And I don't want breakfast."

"Yes, it's patently obvious that you rarely eat," he commented, glancing at her. "But if you work here, you'll need to. You see," he added, leaning back with a disgustingly confident smile on his tanned face, "my grandmother and I have an arrangement about you."

This sounded unpleasant. She sat down gingerly and eyed him suspiciously. "You have?"

"Yes. I don't have a private secretary. And since you'll be here all day, every day—" he made it sound like a waking curse "—and since grandmother will need you for only a few hours a day, we've decided to share you."

Her skin chilled. "I don't want to be shared."

"But then, it isn't your choice," he reminded her. "You can always go home and marry Henry," he suggested mildly.

She shuddered delicately. "Even working for you wouldn't be that bad."

"Should I be flattered?" he murmured dryly. He lifted his head, craggy features relaxing a little as he studied her face. "It must take layers of makeup," he said absently.

He surprised her. "What?" she stammered.

"Your complexion," he explained. "It's much too perfect to be natural."

"I use soap," she said curtly. "Nothing else, not even powder. I don't like artificial things."

"Neither do I," he returned. His tanned fingers toyed with a spoon in his coffee. He was wearing a blue jacket with a white shirt and a speckled tie, and he looked every inch a business magnate. But the muscles under that jacket were formidable, and they rippled with every movement he made. His hair seemed even darker under the light, neat and clean, and there was a faint darkness where he shaved, as if he needed to shave often. His mouth fascinated her. She kept remembering how it felt on hers, how expert it had been. He was the kind of man who could have had any woman he wanted, and she was secretly glad that her powers of resistance weren't going to be tested by him. She would have been defenseless in any kind of confrontation, and she wouldn't have the sophistication to hold him. He could have broken her heart, and she was delighted that he wasn't going to try.

"She's very fragile," she ventured as she poured coffee from the carafe into a delicate china cup and added cream.

"What?"

"Your grandmother," she returned. "How did she break her hip?"

"Trying to learn how to break dance."

Amelia had just taken a mouthful of coffee and almost strangled on it. She gaped at him.

"That's right," he said calmly. He sipped his own coffee. "She had videotapes of the steps, and she was trying to do a spin. She was too close to the fireplace. She went down on the stone hearth."

"But she's seventy-five!" she exclaimed.

"She likes hard rock," he continued. "She enjoys very racy movies, she flirts outrageously with men, she can outdrink me when she likes and you'll get an education in the art of self-expression if you're ever in the vicinity when she loses her temper."

She was only just getting her breath back. "An exceptional lady," she said.

"Quite. But she has an unusually soft heart, and I don't want her hurt," he added, with a level, hard gaze. "I don't know you. But I will. And if I find out anything that doesn't jibe with what information you've given me, I will toss you out on your ear."

She met his hard gaze levelly, eyebrows raised. "Well, I did get a parking ticket once," she confessed.

"Funny girl," he taunted.

"My mama says that laughing beats crying any day," she returned with a vacant smile.

"Laugh while you can," he said pleasantly. He finished his coffee. "Are you through? I'd like to get started."

She blinked. "Started doing what?"

"Working, of course. I'm going out in the field today, to inspect a potential building site. You'll come along and take notes."

"But...but, Mrs. Carson...?"

He got to his feet, towering over her. "Grandmother won't be up for hours yet. She watched movies until four in the morning."

"But she said to be here at eight-thirty," she protested.

"I told you she'd be trying her hand at matchmaking," he reminded her.

She looked him up and down and tried to manage a disparaging expression. "Well, I'm really sorry, Wentworth, but you aren't my type. I don't like big men."

He pursed his lips and smiled mischievously. "No?" He reached out a big hand and tugged her gently to her feet. His hands caught her waist and lifted her on a level with his eyes. "There are advantages to being my size. I don't get argued with much."

Her hands were on his big shoulders, cold and nervous. And the proximity disturbed her so much that she could feel her heart beating. His eyes were almost black, with very definite whites and black rims around the brown. They were impressive eyes. His nose was impressive, too, despite its size. It had a faintly Roman look, very straight and formidable. His forehead was broad and his mouth was firm and his chin had a dimple in it. She'd never liked dimpled chins, but this one was really sexy.

"Were any of your people Italian?" she asked without meaning to.

"Yes, as a matter of fact," he said. "My grandfather was."

"You...look Roman."

His mouth curved a little, making the dimple pronounced. "So they tell me." His hands contracted, bringing her closer, so that her face was under his, her mouth was under his, so that she could breathe the coffee he'd just swallowed. "Why did you take the job?"

He was really unsettling her. She could feel the warmth of his breath on her lips, the steely strength in the hands that held her off the floor so effortlessly. "I...needed it," she whispered.

"There are other employers in Chicago," he reminded her.

"How...far would I get without a recommendation?"

He searched her darkening blue eyes. "Not far," he said, relenting. "Your eyes looked blue yesterday. Now they're gray."

"Are they?"

One corner of his mouth twitched. "Do I make you nervous, Miss Glenn?" he taunted in a voice like velvet. His eyes dropped to her lips.

"Don't play with me," she whispered shakily.

"But you said you wanted someone to play with," he reminded her. "Only yesterday, in fact, as you were driving away in that yellow boxcar you own."

"It isn't a boxcar. And I didn't mean this kind of playing."

His mouth bent closer to hers as he eased her down to her feet again. "Didn't you? Most women today play at love."

"I'm not most women, and I don't know how to," she said. She tugged against his hands. "Let me go."

"Afraid of me?" he chided gently.

She met his dark eyes. "I'm not in your league, Worth. Don't do this to me. I'm no threat to your grandmother, or to you."

"I'm not sure about the latter, Amy," he said quietly, and the sound of her name on his lips had an oddly sweet sound. He bent a little more and brushed his hard mouth softly against hers, a whisper of sensation that tantalized more than satisfied. He lifted his dark, shaggy head, and studied her confused expression.

"Where are we going, and what do you want me to do?" she asked.

He let her go. "To the north side, to see a parcel of land I'm interested in developing. And I want you to take down some ideas and estimates for me. I can't get the hang of dictating into a tape recorder. I don't trust the damned things anyway. You can take dictation?" he added with a sharp glance.

"Yes," she said. "I can. But I don't have a pad or pen...."

"Come with me."

She followed him, taking two steps for every one of his, and feeling oddly like a midget beside him. He made her feel wildly feminine. It was a sensation she wasn't sure she liked.

He led her into a pine-paneled office with a huge oak desk and heavy furniture with leather upholstery. It had a stone fireplace and a thick beige carpet and dark brown curtains. A man's room. It intimidated her, like its owner.

He jerked open a desk drawer and produced a steno pad and two pencils and handed them to her. She tucked them into her shoulder bag while he watched her with narrowed, speculating eyes. She kept her eyes lowered so that he couldn't see the confusion he'd caused. She had to remember that he didn't want her there, and that he might use underhanded means to remove her. If only she didn't view those means with anticipation as well as fear!

When they got to the garage, he went immediately to the Mercedes and she gave him a quick glance. She'd expected him to get into the Rolls.

"The Rolls belongs to my grandmother," he told her with a knowing smile as he opened the passenger door of the Mercedes for her. "She likes elegance and style. I prefer subtlety and performance." As he said it, he gave her own pitifully aging relic a hard glare.

"The yardman told me to put it in here," she said icily. "I guessed that you wouldn't want it standing in your front yard. It might shock some of your friends."

"Most of my friends are dead or out of the country," he said carelessly, getting in beside her. He cranked the car and reversed it smoothly out of the garage. "I thought you might appreciate having it out of the weather. I don't give a damn if you park it in front of the mailbox."

She shifted restlessly. "Sorry." Her eyes searched his profile, liking the strength of it. It wasn't the epitome of male beauty, but it was a strong, earthy face, full of complexities. Like the man.

"Are you an only child?" he asked as he drove.

"Yes. Are you?"

He shook his head. "I had a brother, two years younger. He was killed in Vietnam, about half a mile from where I was stationed at Da Nang."

"I'm sorry." She stared at the purse in her lap. "It must have been hard on your grandmother, too."

"She grieved for a long time. Jackie was full of fun. He teased her, brought her flowers. He was always into something exciting. She lived through him." His chest rose and fell gently. "I was never able to replace him in her eyes. I'm not as uninhibited. I work harder than I play."

"I can just see you, trying to break dance," she murmured.

He laughed. "I'd go through the floor," he said with a dry glance in her direction.

She measured the size of him and silently agreed. "What are you going to build?" she asked.

"At the new site? A condominium."

"Another one?" she exclaimed. "But Chicago is full of condominiums."

"Not in this part of town," he countered. "This one is specifically for elderly residents. A sort of low-cost condo."

"Don't tell me you have a soft spot, too?" she teased gently.

He glanced at her as they stopped for a red light. "Only for grandmother. So look out, if you have ideas in that direction. I gave up dreams of a wife and kids a long time ago. I'm not in the market for an over-the-hill virgin."

Her indrawn breath was audible over traffic. "What makes you think I'd ever be interested in you, Mount Everest!"

"You like kissing me," he said carelessly, and had the audacity to grin.

"I like popcorn, too, so what?" she demanded.

His dark eyes skimmed over her body before he moved into the throng of early-morning traffic again. "So you're curious. Maybe I am, too."

"About what?" she had to ask.

His mouth curved. "Sex."

She turned her gaze out the window at the skyscrapers and city traffic and blaring horns. "I imagine you've already forgotten everything I'll learn for the rest of my life."

"I was a rounder in my youth," he admitted. "And once or twice, things got serious. But I had great instincts for self-preservation."

There was an odd note in his deep, gravelly voice, and she turned her head in time to catch the tautening of his jaw. "And someone hurt you, really badly," she said without thinking.

The black scowl would have intimidated her if they hadn't been moving. "Has grandmother been talking to you?" he demanded.

"Not about your private life, no," she returned. Her eyes fell to her lap. "I almost got engaged once. He was a nice guy. Very flashy, good family, old money." She smiled bitterly. "We got on like a house on fire. I would have done anything for him. First love and all that. He was proper about it, though, he wanted to marry me, not seduce me. So he took me home to mother. I was nineteen and in my second year of college." She stretched and studied the couple in a cab across from them as he made a turn.

"Obviously you didn't marry him," he said, breaking the silence.

"His mother was horrified. I was a little country girl from Georgia, and I looked it. I won't bore you with the details. Suffice it to say that after a week at his home, suffering his mother's contempt and getting a look at his way of life, I broke the engagement myself and came home. I quit college. I couldn't bear the memories. It took me a long time to get over it."

"He was a mama's boy, I gather."

She nodded. "I heard later that he married the heiress to a cosmetic company. A nice little merger."

"Too bad it didn't work out."

"On the contrary," she said. "I was lucky. He drank like a fish and did everything his mother told him. Retrospect is a wonderful thing. I'd have had a horrendous life. After the newness had worn off, I'd have died of neglect. He wasn't even much as a would-be lover," she added with a shy laugh. "He grabbed."

"Men can be taught," he said with a sideways glance. "None of us know without being told what pleases a woman. Despite the fiction that says we should."

"I'd never be able to do that," she said. Her long legs crossed as she shifted to face him. It was uncanny how easy he was to talk to. She might have known him all her life.

"Why not?"

She leaned her head on the seat, adjusting her seat belt so that she had enough room. The leather seat was plush and comfortable, and the air-conditioning made the already formidable heat bearable. "Oh, I'd be too shy," she said, smiling dreamily. "I can't imagine taking my clothes off in front of a man."

His heavy eyebrows lifted. "How do you imagine people make love, in dark closets?"

"At night, of course, with the lights out," she said.

He looked up toward the headliner. "My God!"

"Well, don't they?"

"I am not licensed to teach sex."

She actually flushed and quickly turned back toward the window. She hadn't realized how intimate the conversation was getting. Flustered, she searched around for a safe topic.

"How much farther is it to your building site?" she asked. "I don't think I've ever actually seen anything in the planning stages. Do you have blueprints or...?"

"Stop floundering," he said gently. "I didn't mean to snap at you."

The gentleness was unexpected. And unwelcome. It made her vulnerable, and she couldn't let that happen. Her chin lifted. "No harm done. What about the building?"

He pulled up at another traffic light and stared at her. "Fascinating," he murmured. "I can actually see the wall going up. I thought I was the only one who did that."

"Did what?" she asked tightly.

"Never mind." He reached out and touched her hair lightly, noticing the way she tensed and the panicky look in the blue eyes that searched his accusingly. "Why are you nervous?"

"It's disturbing to sit so close to the enemy," she countered.

He smiled faintly. "Is it?"

"The light's changing," she remarked.

"Evasive maneuvers?" he taunted. But he turned back to the steering wheel, and the tension was broken.

The building site was only minutes further along. He'd turned on the news and they'd listened to that for the rest of the drive.

Amelia wasn't sure what she'd expected to find. A nice level lot, probably. But what they found was a deserted tenement, old and crumbling, on a corner lot.

"Where are you going to put your condo," she asked, "under it or on top?"

He laughed at her expression. "We're going to take this building down and clear off the lot first."

"Isn't that expensive?"

"Of course. Construction always is." He parked the car at the curb and helped her out, his eyes narrow and keen as he studied the lay of the land.

"Have you already bought this?" she asked.

"If I had, why would I be here looking at it, for God's sake?" he shot at her.

She drew herself up to her full height, still much inferior to his own. "You have a black temper," she told him curtly.

He folded his arms across his broad chest and studied her quietly. "Go ahead. Point out my shortcomings. Don't be bashful."

"You're overbearing," she obliged. "Insolent, arrogant, insensitive..."

He glanced at his watch. "I only have another hour before I'm due at a trustee's meeting."

"...maddening and hardheaded," she concluded agreeably.

"Fine," he replied. "Now. How would you like a thumbnail sketch of your own shortcomings?"

"I don't have any," she informed him smugly. "I am courteous, friendly, kind, thoughtful, cheerful and an asset to the world."

He looked as if he was trying not to laugh, but the absurdity of the pat answer got to him. He turned away, his shoulders shaking.

Amelia got out her pad and pen and tried to look professional. "Would you like to take notes?"

He stuck his hands in his pockets and glanced down at her. "Why, am I supposed to write a testimonial for you?"

"About the building site! That is why you brought me along, isn't it?"

"Oh. That." He glanced up and around. "Let's go walking."

He started off down the street. She almost had to run to keep up with him, aware of city smells and sounds, and longing halfheartedly for her home and the crash of the Atlantic against a shimmering white beach and the cry of sea gulls.

"Where are you going?" she asked breathlessly. Her high heels were uncomfortable, much too high and spiked.

He studied her feet. "Why do you wear those things? Do you like risking your neck every time you move?"

"They're stylish," she defended.

"They're stupid. Next time, wear flats."

"How was I supposed to know I was going to be press-ganged into an expedition at the breakfast table?" she wanted to know.

"I suppose you were looking forward to tea and cakes and polite conversation, with an occasional scribbled letter from grandmother to give you the illusion of working?" he prompted.

"Your grandmother does need someone with her," she said angrily. The morning was hot, and her temper wasn't helping. She pushed at a loose strand of dark hair. "Except for the maid, most of the staff are almost retirement age. What if she fell?"

His face hardened. "You aren't a nurse," he said.

"I was a nurse's aide," she informed him. "I've done a lot of odd jobs in my life, and that was one of them. At least I know first aid. And surely she does need a secretary to help her do things?''

He stopped in the middle of the block and glared down at her. He wasn't contradicting her, though.

"I can give you three or four character references," she continued. "Two of them are ministers, one in the city and one back home. About the only illegal thing I've ever done in my life was to jaywalk. And in Seagrove, in tourist season, that is really an act of valor more than a crime." Her blue eyes in her softly tanned face held his. "I'll start looking for another job in the morning," she promised. "Just let me stay with her until I find one. Is that fair enough?"

"All right," he said, relenting. His eyes narrowed.

"I know." She sighed. "You don't trust me. My grandfather wouldn't trust you, either," she added with a grin. "He thinks Chicago is full of gangsters. He wouldn't speak to Dad and Mom for days after I left home to come here. He even calls me sometimes to make sure I haven't been the victim of a gang murder."

He smiled in spite of himself. "Flinty character, I gather?"

"A real hell-raiser," she agreed. "He was a fisherman until times got hard and he lost his boat. He retired and now he does odd jobs. He hasn't been the same since my grandmother died. He said it took the color out of the world for him."

"What did she die of?"

"A heart attack. It was quick. And kind of nice, if death can be called that, because she died working in her flower garden. It was what she loved most." She smiled and had to fight tears. It had only been a year, and the hurt was raw sometimes. "My other grandparents, my father's parents, died years ago. I never knew them. Mom's parents have been like a second set for me. Dad and I could never talk the way Granddad and I can."

"Was it a happy marriage, your grandparents'?" he asked.

She smiled. "They'd just celebrated their fiftieth wedding anniversary. He took her to a drive-in movie afterward and they came home with the windows fogged up," she added with a mischievous look. "You always had to knock before you went into the house. They liked variety, and once mama walked in on them in the living room."

"My God," he said with a laugh.

"They were very modern grandparents." She walked along beside him, remembering. "Your grandmother is very like mine. I like her."

"So do I." He pulled a package of cigarettes from his pocket and stared at it. The cellophane had never been opened.

She glanced up. She didn't remember seeing him with a cigarette. "Do you smoke?" she asked suddenly.

"Yes and no." He sighed and repocketed the package. "I've been off them for two weeks."

"Cold turkey?"

He nodded. "I need something to do with my hands."

"You might take up knitting, I hear it's very...no!" She dodged as he aimed a swipe at her. "Gentlemen don't hit ladies!"

"I'm from Chicago, not the South," he reminded her.

"I know," she replied. "Your accent gives you away every time."

"I don't have an accent."

Her eyebrows lifted wildly. "If I took you home with me, people would come from miles around just to listen to you talk."

"You're one to talk about accents," he chided with a mocking glance.

"Well, I don't have one," she drawled. "Not in Georgia, at least."

He shook his head. His eyes were busy, staring around, measuring, calculating.

"What are we looking for?" she asked.

"I'll tell you when I find it. Write this down."

He dictated and she scribbled as they walked. He noted locations of grocery stores, bus stops, drugstores, businesses, traffic lights, streets, until Amelia got lost in the tangle. As they got around the block and back to the potential site, he was still throwing out ideas.

He looked up at the tenement and had her write down names of potential subcontractors, demolition people, city government officials, building inspectors. Then he made notes about the site itself, using terms she had to ask him to spell. It became obvious that he knew his business.

"I'll want cost estimates, too," he murmured to himself. "I'll send Reynolds out here with the blueprints."

"Cost estimates?"

He looked down at her. "I have to know everything when I start a project. Right down to the cost of each nail I'm going to use."

"How do you do that?" she asked, genuinely curious.

"If you're really interested, I'll tell you over lunch."

"I'd like that."

She expected him to drive her back to the house, but he took her instead to the very elegant French restaurant where she'd been arrested. Chez Pierre.

"No," she pleaded as he opened the door for her at the entrance and handed the keys to a parking valet.

"Yes," he said firmly. "Come on. They'll never recognize you."

They didn't, either. Not even the hostess who'd been so startled. They were shown to a cozy table for two by a window overlooking a flowery courtyard.

"Lovely!" she exclaimed, sighing over the profusion of flowers. "I love flowers!"

"Yes, I puzzled that out."

She looked across the table at him, eyes wide and curious.

"It was the way you spoke about your grandmother's flowers," he explained.

"I like growing things," she confessed with a sigh. "Except that I've got no place to do it. My apartment is surrounded by green hedges and lush grass, and the Kennedys have terrible hay fever. I wouldn't dream of inflicting pollen on them. They've been good to me."

"Your landlords, I gather?"

She nodded. "They were trying to live on their retirement pension, without much success, so they gave in to necessity and rented their garage apartment. I applied, and I guess they thought I was harmless. I've lived there ever since I've been in Chicago."

"It's tidy," he said.

"It's tiny," she corrected, laughing. "But I can walk to the beach on weekends."

"I imagine you miss the coast?" he asked.

She nodded. "I miss shelling and sitting on the beach and watching the Atlantic in full storm," she said softly, her eyes brimming with excitement. "You can see whitecaps to the horizon. It's noisy and wet, and the wind rips into your hair like a comb, stinging your eyes." She drew in a breath. "I miss it."

He was watching her, toying with his silverware. "Yes," he said absently, "you do seem the kind of woman who'd risk a hurricane to stand on a deserted beach. I imagine you like to stand out in electrical storms as well."

She laughed self-consciously. "Granddad says I'm an elemental person. So is he. Not foolhardy, exactly, just adventurous."

"And passionate," he added, holding her eyes. "Ten to one you're a fire sign."

"If you mean astrology, I'm Sagittarius."

He laughed softly. "Freedom-loving, adventurous, outdoorsy, passionate."

"How did you know?"

"I'm Sagittarius myself."

"I'd have guessed Leo."

He shook his head. "I was a Christmas child. My birthday is Christmas eve. When's yours?"

"The day after yours. I was a Christmas present."

He laughed. "Ironic."

"I'd rather be a May baby," she said with a sigh. "I like emeralds."

"But turquoise would suit you better," he remarked. "It's the old December birthstone. I prefer it."

She glanced at his hands. They were big and darkly tanned, and rippling with strength. He wore only one ring—a huge silver one with a square turquoise setting—on the little finger of his right hand.

"I hadn't noticed before," she said.

He glanced at her own hands. "You don't wear jewelry at all," he said, and seemed surprised.

"I have a class ring, but I never wear it. I'm too careless. I lose things."

The waiter came with menus, and Amelia chose a steak and salad. So did he.

"Protein," he said. "I like red meat."

"Raw red meat, judging by the way you're having it cooked," she laughed.

He leaned forward. "It's hard to get a tough rare steak, didn't you know? Some of the better-cooked cuts bounce."

So he wasn't such a stuffed shirt as she'd thought. All through the meal, he was courteous, attentive and interesting to talk to. He explained the notes he'd had her take, and the preliminary steps that construction required. He answered her questions and satisfied her curiosity. And she was reluctant to see their excursion end. It had been unexpectedly pleasant.

His grandmother was waiting in the living room when they got back.

"So there you are." She glared at Wentworth from the sofa, where she was lounging in a breezy pantsuit. "Absconding with my new companion on her first day, working her to death so she'll quit!"

"We agreed," he reminded her with a grin and a quick kiss on her smooth forehead. "She's all yours now." He glanced at Amelia, who had collapsed into a big armchair and was debating whether or not she could get away with taking off her shoes. "I'll need those notes tomorrow morning."

"Oh! Your trustees' meeting!" she exclaimed suddenly.

"Damn!" he burst out. "I forgot all about it. I'd better call."

He left the room and Jeanette Carson laughed delightfully. "That's a first," she told Amelia in a conspiratorial whisper. "He never forgets meetings. What did you do to him?"

"I asked him how to build things," she said simply. "It was really interesting."

"I've always thought so." Jeanette sighed. She leaned back. "Well, dear, what shall we do today? I thought we might sunbathe and listen to the radio."

"I don't have a bathing suit, but I'd like to sit in the sun," Amelia said. She gave her employer a wry glance, remembering what Worth had told her. "What kind of music do you like."

"I like Bruce Springsteen and Lionel Ritchie and Michael Jackson and Prince," she said.

"Thank God," Amelia said with a sigh. "My favorites."

Jeanette laughed delightedly. "My dear, you and I are going to be great friends. Here, help me up, and let's escape before Worth comes back and captures you. You can work up those notes before dinner."

"I really need to leave about six," Amelia ventured.

"Whenever. I'll make sure you have time to do what you need to do for Worth. Come."

Amelia wondered if she should mention that she'd promised Worth that she'd start looking for another job tomorrow. With a heartfelt sigh she went out after the elderly lady. It was going to be harder to quit this job than she'd expected. Even though she'd only known the Carsons for a couple of days, it would be like giving up family. How odd, she told herself, that she should think of them that way.

Five

The next morning Worth was gone when Amelia got to the house. While she was waiting for Mrs. Carson to wake up, she began to run through the Help Wanted columns, as she'd promised Worth she would. He'd made it patently obvious that he didn't want her around, despite his grandmother's wishes. And Amelia didn't really have the stomach to make a cat-and-dog fight of it. That wouldn't do anybody any good, especially Jeanette Carson.

She found two promising offers and quietly dialed the numbers. The first job had already been filled, she was told, and someone had forgotten to cancel the ad. But the second was still available, and she was given an appointment to apply for it the next day. She hung up, feeling hopeful. It was secretarial work in a law office, and she thought she might like it.

Worth had rushed off to his trustees' meeting the previous afternoon and had still been gone when she left that night. Mrs. Carson had coaxed her to leave the transcribing of her notes for this morning. Now she went to work on them. She finished and put them on Worth's desk, just as Mrs. Carson came easing in on her walker. The old lady was dressed in Bermuda shorts and a loose top with a trendy red scarf around her silver curls.

"There you are." She laughed. "Well, I'm finally awake. There was this great murder mystery on cable early this morning, and I just had to watch it."

"You don't get enough rest," Amelia teased gently.

"Rest!" Mrs. Carson scoffed. "I'm seventy-five years old. Who wants to rest at my age? I'm headed for the Big Sleep, you know, Amy. I'll get my rest then. For now, I'm going to do everything I always shied away from when I was younger. I'm going to live my last years."

Amelia smiled warmly. "Tough, aren't you?" she said with a grin.

"Tough as old combat boots," came the laughing reply. "I was a police reporter, my dear. That is not a job for a cream puff."

"Amen." Amelia went forward to open the door out onto the patio.

"Why don't you dress comfortably?" Jeanette asked gently, eyeing her young companion's neat green dress, high heels and businesslike hairstyle. "You make me feel like a corporate executive. Wear slacks tomorrow and let your hair down, Amy."

"You wouldn't mind?" Amelia asked. "But Worth…"

"Worth is not your boss, I am. Besides, he'll be out of our hair for a couple of weeks. He's going to build me a condo," she said, chuckling as they sat down on loungers and waited among the blooming flowers for lunch to be served at a neat little white table with a glass top.

"Is it yours?" she asked.

"No." Jeanette sighed. "But I'd love to have one of the units, really I would. Then maybe I could do as I please without having Worth watch me like a hawk. Jackie was so different," she murmured, deep in thought. "A free spirit, like me."

"Your other grandson?"

Jeanette's pale eyes stabbed at her. "How did you know?"

"Worth told me."

She relaxed against the lounger. "Yes, Jackie was a wild boy. But Worth is kind and considerate, and when he forgets to be the boss, he's good company. We have our spats. He's hot tempered like me, and he likes his own way. I just wish he took more time for himself. That company will kill him some day."

"I suppose it takes the place of wife and children," Amelia thought aloud.

"Yes, it does." Jeanette sighed again. "I tried matchmaking for a while, you know, after Connie left him. But he hasn't wanted any kind of commitment. I feel responsible for that."

Amelia wanted desperately to ask, but she hesitated, not wanting to pry either.

Jeanette saw the question in her eyes. "Connie was a secretary. Years younger than Worth. He had money, and she wanted to live in luxury. He bought her diamonds and furs, he gave her a car. But I saw through her, and I made the mistake of saying so. She turned on me like a tigress," she added on a bitter laugh, "and figured she was going to have to get me out of the way before she had a clear field with Worth."

"You don't mean that," Amelia said quickly.

"Don't I?" Jeanette said. She studied the frank shock on the younger woman's face. "No, she hadn't planned to murder me. But she spent every available moment when we were alone, telling me how much she wanted me out of the house. She did everything, in fact, except take an ad in the *Times*. Worth didn't know. He loved her, you see, and despite my own feelings, I didn't want to hurt him." The old eyes clouded with memory. "When I wouldn't be budged, she found more subtle ways of tormenting me. Breaking my little treasures. Making remarks about how sickly I looked. Finally I couldn't stand it anymore, and I had to speak to Worth." She took a slow breath.

"And he didn't believe me, Amy. He knew I didn't like Connie, so he thought it was jealousy."

"He must have loved her very much," Amelia said gently. She could imagine how it would have been. Worth was the kind of man who gave everything, not just pieces, of himself.

"He worshiped her, child," Jeanette said. "I was hurt, but I understood. I told him I'd move out when they were married." Her eyes fell. "The wedding date was finalized. The invitations went out. She bought the wedding dress."

Amelia was sitting on the very edge of her seat. "And then?"

"And then Connie came to see me, the week before the wedding. She didn't know Worth was in the house. She wanted to gloat, to show me that she'd won. She laid it on so thick and upset me so much that I had a heart attack. I'll never forget the way she looked when Worth came in the open door. She tried to justify herself, but he never saw her. He got an ambulance. I came to in the hospital." She stared at her wrinkled hands. "I don't know what was said between them, but the wedding was quietly canceled. Worth has never gotten over the fact that he didn't believe me. I've spent months trying to convince him that it doesn't matter anymore, but he hasn't brought a woman here since. He hasn't gotten involved since. I feel guilty about it and responsible for it, but there's nothing I can do. He can't get past his guilt to another relationship."

"What happened to the woman?" Amelia asked.

"I don't even know," Jeanette said. "I like to think she was eaten by sharks, but we never get exactly what we want, you know. It amazes me how blind men are about women, even the most intelligent men. They can never see through the glitter to the ugliness beneath."

"We're all guilty of not wanting to see ugliness," Amelia reminded her.

Jeanette smiled, and her eyes sparkled. "I suppose so. Perhaps I've been bitter about it, too. Connie might have been my last hope for great-grandchildren. I'm afraid Worth will never risk his heart again."

Amelia leaned forward. "You could adopt," she whispered.

The older woman started to laugh, the sound rich and soft and delightful in the sunny garden. "You're good for me, child. Don't leave."

Amelia averted her eyes. If everything went according to plan, she would be leaving Jeanette. Fortunately the arrival of their tray in Baxter's immaculate hands saved her from having to admit the truth, that her time here was already ending.

It was after eight o'clock and Amelia was just ready to leave when Worth came in the front door. He looked weary. He was carrying the blue blazer. His shirt was open at the throat, and so thin that Amelia could see his broad chest and the shadow of thick hair over it through the fabric. His slacks were close fitting, emphasizing the powerful muscles of his thighs. In the light of the chandelier, he looked bigger and darker than ever, and his black hair glowed with bluish highlights. He glanced up from a sheet of paper in his hand, noticing her poised in the hall with her light cotton jacket in her hand.

"Did you transcribe my notes?" he asked.

"Yes."

"Where's my grandmother?"

"On the phone," she faltered. "She had a light supper and went to her room, to talk to one of her friends on the phone."

He ran a hand through his hair, and looked for all the world like Clark Gable in *It Happened One Night*. He needed a shave, and he was clearly dragging.

"I...what you asked me to do, I did," she said, moving closer so that she couldn't be overheard.

He stared down into her wide blue eyes for a long moment. "What?"

"I think I've found another job," she said, and tried her best to look happy about it. "It's a secretarial position in a law office. I have an interview in the morning."

"Are you bored already?" he shot at her.

"You told me to look for something else," she said indignantly.

He sighed angrily. "She's gotten used to you," he said. "I'd have hell for a month if I let you go now."

She couldn't seem to find the right words. She searched his weary face and wanted so much to touch him, to soothe him. He looked as if someone had already given him hell.

"Such expressive eyes," he murmured. He moved nearer, a giant close up, and reached down with his free hand to cup her chin. "Feeling sorry for me, Amy?" he asked with a tired smile.

"You look as if you've been run over," she said, and her voice was softer than she meant it to be.

"I feel it. I've been meeting with city officials. Try that on an empty stomach."

"There are some cold cuts in the kitchen, left over from supper."

He searched her eyes quietly. "Have you eaten?" he asked.

She had to swallow down a denial, because she wanted to stay with him. "Yes," she said, and wondered if you could call the tiny salad she'd shared with her employer a meal. "I have to get home. I'm expecting a phone call."

"All right." He released her and watched as she walked to the door.

She stopped with her hand on the doorknob and glanced worriedly over her shoulder. He looked so alone.

His eyes went dark even at the distance, holding her to the spot. "Baxter quits at eight," he said. "So does the maid and the yardman. Nobody lives in." It was eight-thirty now; Amy had gotten into a long conversation with Jeanette and hadn't been able to find a graceful way to leave.

Worth dropped his jacket and tie into an elegant wing chair in the hall and flicked open his shirt, as if the heat bothered him. In the opening, she could see a thick shock of black hair, a blatantly masculine sight that made her heart run away. "I suppose I can do without dinner," he murmured, glancing at her.

As if he knew, she thought, turning back from the door, that her soft heart couldn't let him go without eating.

"I can fix you something," she said.

"What about the phone call you're expecting?" he asked with narrowed eyes and a faint smile.

Her eyes lowered to his chest. "I didn't want to impose."

"You won't be. I hate eating alone."

He turned and she followed him into the spacious kitchen, which was done in white and pale yellow with old-fashioned overhead fans. She opened the refrigerator and took out cold cuts, quickly fashioning a meal from salad and ham and sliced bread.

She made coffee and had a ham sandwich of her own while it perked. She poured the steaming coffee into delicate rose-patterned china and watched his big fingers try to manage the dainty thing.

"You need a huge mug," she murmured on a smile. "To fit your hands."

"They aren't that big," he said, chuckling. He reached one out and caught hers in it, studying the difference in size. Her slender fingers seemed small in his, and she could feel the strength in that callused warmth. He had beautifully masculine hands, olive tan with flat, immaculate nails and wrists that were darkly sprinkled with hair.

"You're very hairy," she remarked without thinking as her eyes lifted to his chest, where the shirt had come open when he leaned toward her.

"All over," he returned, watching her flush. "Don't you like hairy men, Miss Glenn?"

She tried to draw her hand back, but his locked into it, fingers between fingers in a lazy, sensuous movement.

"I don't know," she faltered.

He leaned back in the chair, tugging at her hand. "Then why don't you come here and we'll find out together."

Lord, he was strong! She found herself pulled out of the chair before she could protest, and drawn toward him. Arrogant beast, sitting there like Caesar, smiling confidently, muscles rippling as he overcame her resistance.

"Mr. Carson..." she began.

He tugged at her hand, landing her squarely on his lap. Under her, his powerfully muscled thighs rippled as he shifted her so that her cheek was against his upper arm, so that her view of the world ended at his face. He smelled of cologne, something musky and oriental, and he laughed like a predator at her blank stare.

"Now, feel," he said, sliding her hand inside his shirt. He pressed it palm down into the thick tangle of hair. "Hairy as hell."

It wasn't fair, she thought, staring up at him. She was melting, and no amount of willpower was going to spare her. Her lips parted as she experienced for the first time in her life the powerful sensuality of touch. He moved her hand, watching her as he taught her how to stroke him.

"Yes, that's it," he said on a soft laugh, "I like being touched. Especially like this," he added, his voice like velvet, and he guided her hand down toward the flat plane of his stomach.

"No!" she whispered, tugging back her hand as it touched his belt.

"How you do bristle with inhibitions, Miss Glenn," he observed calculatingly.

"I haven't asked for private tutoring," she said, flustered.

"No, you haven't, big eyes," he admitted, searching her face with oddly patient eyes. "But I think you could use a bit, all the same."

"I'll hire a gigolo," she promised. "Please let me go."

"Why?" He drew her hand back to his chest and held it there. "I'm not asking you for anything. Yet."

"Ever," she corrected. "I work for your grandmother, and only temporarily. My duties don't include satisfying your appetite."

"I don't think you could, Amy," he said shockingly. "You wouldn't have the slightest idea how, would you?"

"No, I wouldn't," she said irritably. "For which you should thank God. At least, I won't be chasing after you!"

His thumb brushed across her lips and he studied them intently for a long time. "Why not?" he asked softly. "I might enjoy being chased by you."

"Well, I wouldn't enjoy it," she muttered, trying to break the light but steely hold that big arm had around her shoulders. "And will you stop treating me like a new toy?"

"That isn't how I think of you at all," he said under his breath. "Not at all." His hand moved up to her bun and began removing pins. She tried to stop him and only managed to pull out a few long, dark hairs in the process, so she gave up. He laid the bobby pins on the table and smoothed her hair down over her shoulders, as if he loved its silky length.

"It feels like satin," he said quietly, stroking it. "I'd forgotten how sensuous long hair can be."

"Been dating bald women, have we?" she said with a nervous laugh. "You've had your fun, now suppose you let me go home?"

His hand moved around to her face, devastating as it traced her soft skin and touched her bow of a mouth. His dark eyes were devoid of laughter now; intent and searching and curious. "You don't look twenty-eight," he told her. He bent his head. "I want you, Amy."

Before she could find a sensible answer, his warm mouth was covering hers. She wanted to protest, but she liked what he was doing too much. His lips coaxed hers to part for him, to allow the slow, rhythmic penetration of his tongue. Her fingers clenched in the thick hair over his chest, and he stiffened.

"Yes," he whispered against her lips, "yes, I like that. Do it again."

Her eyes opened, gray as a rainy day as they searched his. Her fingers contracted and he smiled. It was a kind of smile she barely remembered from her disastrous near-engagement, a possessive and totally male look that hinted of conquest, delighted dominance. She should have resented it, but he was the kind of man who made arrogance seem natural.

She watched as his mouth came back to hers, tenderly probing, teasing. Her body reacted restlessly to the building passion, moving against his involuntarily.

"You feel it now, don't you?" he whispered. His free hand moved to her back and turned her into his body, so that her breasts were pressed against his broad, warm chest. He kissed her, and even as his mouth began taking possession, he moved, so that her breasts were drawn back and forth against him, so that the tips became sensitive and began to harden. Her blouse and bra were thin and his shirt was completely out of the way now, and when he laughed softly, she knew it was because he could feel what had happened to her.

"This is delicious," he whispered. His mouth slid down to her throat, and he inhaled the flowery scent of her skin while he learned the delicate lines with his lips. "You even taste like a virgin," he breathed, drawing his tongue along the throbbing pulse under the warm skin.

Her face turned into his shoulder and hid there, because she was vulnerable now and he knew it. She had no secrets from him.

His lips touched her closed eyelids, nudging her face out of hiding. "Amy..." he murmured as he found her mouth again.

This time, there was no teasing. He arched her body against his, and the pressure of his hard mouth forced her head down into the crook of his elbow. He nudged her mouth open under his and began a devouring, expertly sensual exploration of it that made her tremble and ache in his embrace.

"I'd forgotten how exciting it could be, to kiss," he whispered against her yielding lips. "I could get drunk on your mouth."

"Don't stop," she heard herself moan.

"How could I," he murmured, his breath loud as he bent again, "when I'm as hungry as you are?"

His arms contracted, and for a long time she fed on his mouth, liking its hard warmth, even liking the bristles where he needed another shave, her arms around his neck now, her body pressed so closely to his that she could feel his heart slamming against her through the muscular walls of his chest. She tasted him, tasted coffee and spice, and opened her mouth even more, so that he could take whatever he liked.

"If I took you," he whispered into her mouth, "would your body open to me so hungrily?"

She moaned, and his mouth grew demanding, his arms began to bruise her against his. With unexpected abandon, she dragged her chest against his so that he could feel how wildly she wanted him, and his hand caught in her long hair as he tugged her head back to look at her face.

His eyes were narrow and glazed with passion, his jaw taut. He let his gaze move down to her breasts, and his free hand began at the top of her dress. He opened the first button, and the second, holding her eyes now, daring her to protest, to stop him.

"I'm going to bare you to the waist, Amy," he said quietly. "And I'm going to feed on you, with my eyes and my mouth."

She was trembling wildly now, with no thought of denying him what she wanted so desperately. Her body arched toward him, yielding, hungry. She could barely breathe for the hunger. And just as he reached the button between her lace-clad breasts, a door opened somewhere down the hall.

Without thinking, she pulled free of his arms and got to her feet, fumbling buttons into holes.

He leaned back and stared at her as she struggled to smooth ruffled hair and straighten her dress. Something dark and soft lingered in the eyes she didn't see. He reached out and retrieved her hairpins.

"Here," he said gently. "Don't forget these."

"Thanks." She took them, meeting his dark eyes.

His fingers caressed hers as he handed over the pins. "Forget that interview tomorrow," he said. "Stay."

She met his eyes. "Worth, I won't sleep with you," she said, putting it bluntly as the footsteps came closer.

"All right," he replied easily.

She shifted, her gaze going toward the door. "I..."

"I won't back you into a corner," he promised. "I can't offer you a future, Amy. And since I can't, I won't compromise you. Is that word old-fashioned enough, or should I say that I won't—" and he used the modern vernacular, and grinned wickedly when she glared at him.

"You have a horrible mouth," she shot, brushing back her long, tangled hair.

"Yours is exquisite," he returned, glancing at it wistfully. "I've never kissed anything so soft and sweet."

"I'm going home," she muttered. She got her purse and started out the door, almost colliding with Jeanette.

"Hello, dear." The older lady grinned. "I thought you'd gone. Worth, Clara wants me to come over for bridge tomorrow night, will you drive me?"

"Of course," he said.

Jeanette looked from one of them to the other. "No arguing," she told them firmly, mistaking the tension. "And don't you dare try to run her off, Worth, or I'll put myself in a nursing home!"

"God forbid, they'd expel you by the third day," Worth said with lazy good humor.

"Hmph!" she grumbled, and smiled at Amelia. "I'll see you tomorrow, dear. Good night."

"Good night," Amelia said, and smiled back.

She didn't even glance at Worth, but was thankful her legs didn't fold on the way out the door.

She lay awake for a long time that night, thinking about the delicious interlude in his arms. She'd wanted him to open her dress, she'd wanted him to look at her and touch her. She'd trembled with hungers she barely understood. Was she crazy to agree to stay on? He'd promised not to compromise her, but what would she do if he put pressure on her? She couldn't refuse him if he kept kissing her. She wanted him.

And what did he want? An interlude or someone to cuddle, but not to keep? Was he being sweet so that she'd stay because his grandmother liked her so much? Or did he just feel sorry for her?

In the end, she decided to live one day at a time and hope for the best. At least she wasn't getting emotionally involved with Worth. That, she couldn't allow. He was not a marrying man, and she couldn't handle an affair. She'd just have to think up some polite way of telling him that she'd rather they had a friendly relationship that didn't get physical. She'd long since given up on the idea of a husband and children, since her relationships were so few and far between, and only lukewarm at best. The good men were married, and the ones who were left were unmarried for too obvious reasons. She'd learned that these days most men liked brief affairs and nothing more lasting. They'd learned that they could have their cake and eat it, too—all the benefits of marriage and none of the responsibilities. But Amy wanted it all, wedding cake and rings and exchanged vows. And she supposed that she'd just waited too long to try. It was too late. She was a spinster for life. Well, so what, she asked herself irritably. Wasn't living alone better than risking everything on a man who could turn out to be a gambler or a secret drunk or a wife beater or a bigamist? Sure it was! She closed her eyes on that optimistic note and finally fell asleep.

Six

Amelia called and canceled her job interview, and settled down at the Carson home, working hours that were odd and sometimes tiring, but enjoying herself all the same.

Worth was in and out, mostly out. Infrequently he had her take notes or type up something for him, but she spent most of her time with Jeanette. The elderly lady could tell some hair-raising stories, recollections of her days as a reporter. Amelia learned about grisly murders and street life with wide-eyed fascination. Jeanette delighted in shocking her.

Summer went into fall, and Amelia found herself looking forward to each new day. The Carson estate had beautiful grounds, and when her employer was busy with other things, she liked to wander around them and sigh over the vegetation. It was a shock when Worth came looking for her one Monday, a day he usually spent at his office.

He'd kept his distance from her since that unexpectedly ardent exchange at the supper table. But he'd been watchful, and in another man she might have mistaken it for interest. She didn't make that mistake with him. Jeanette had told her too much about his past. She'd daydreamed a little, but very quickly she learned that he could turn his emotions on and off, teasing her one minute and bellowing about mistakes the next. She coped with his shifting moods by not letting herself get too involved, by keeping her emotions at a safe distance. And it worked. He became more friend than employer, and she found him unusually easy to talk to, just as she had that first day.

"Does Mrs. Carson want me?" Amelia asked with a smile. She was wearing white slacks with a pink tank top, her hair loose and swinging freely around her shoulders, sandals on her small feet. She laughed as he joined her, and he watched her face for a minute before he replied.

"No," he said lazily. He fell into step beside her. He was wearing gray slacks and a white shirt, rolled up to the elbow and carelessly unbuttoned.

"Something bothering you, boss?" she teased gently.

He glanced down at her with a smile. "No."

"You're home early or going to work late, then," she remarked. She had a strand of grass in her hand, and she nibbled it as they walked back toward the house. It was a beautiful day. Flowers and shrubs bloomed all around the cobblestone path and birds sounded in the tall trees.

"I have something for you," he said.

She stopped walking and stared at him. "For me?"

"Sort of," he murmured dryly. "Come on."

He led her to the side of the house and presented her with a ten-foot square of neatly plowed and raked ground.

Her breath caught. She looked up at him with huge eyes. "For me?" she exclaimed, and her smile was like the sun coming out.

He chuckled at her enthusiasm. "For you. Plant whatever you like."

"Oh, Worth!" Impulsively, without thinking, she barreled into his arms and hugged him fiercely. "Thank you!"

His big hands held her shoulders, held her there, and his head bent over her. "You're more than welcome. It's little enough thanks for the good you've done around here. Grandmother worships you, did you know?"

"It's mutual. I think she's the berries." Amelia sighed. Her eyes closed as she pillowed her cheek against his broad chest. It felt so natural to be held by him, to stand in the shade of the trees and be together. Under her ear, she could hear his heartbeat. At her temples, his breath felt ragged, disturbed.

"Amy," he whispered.

There was a note in his voice that meant trouble. And she wasn't ready to deal with it, not yet. She tugged away from him, smiling to soften the rejection, and folded her arms across her aching breasts. She wouldn't look at him. She couldn't.

"Now, what shall I plant?" she reasoned aloud, oblivious to the strain that colored her unusually high-pitched tone.

He came up behind her, slid his hands around her waist and drew her back so that her body rested on his. "The yardman's name is Harry. He'll get you whatever you like."

"No, really, that isn't necessary, I can buy what I want."

"I said, he'll get it."

"Tyrant."

His hands slid up, so that they rested just under her breasts, and her heartbeat jumped. He felt it and laughed, deep in his throat. "It's broad daylight," he reminded her. "I wouldn't do it in public, if that reassures you."

She knew exactly what he meant, and had to bite her lip to keep from saying something rude. He liked to tease, she knew that by now. He didn't even mean anything by it. She was young and not too unattractive and handy, and he was very much a man. She just had to keep that in mind and everything would be fine.

And it was, until he bent his head and kissed the side of her neck.

She caught her breath and moaned, and everything changed. Very slowly, he turned her, holding her in front of him. He stared down into her eyes so intently and for so long that her heart went wild and she felt as if she were being electrocuted. She jerked her head down against his chest, breathless.

"I've tried," he whispered. "Oh, God, I have."

His hands tightened on her waist. Then, all at once, he bent and lifted her.

She clutched at his shoulders as he turned and carried her into the greenhouse several yards away. It was deserted. The yardman usually took Monday mornings off, and Mrs. Carson was taking her noon nap.

He set her gently down. His big, warm hands framed her face and he searched her eyes. He was breathing heavily, and she could hear his heartbeat.

"I saw a painting of a fairy once," he whispered. "She had long black hair and blue eyes and a slender, beautiful body like yours. And every time I look at you, I want to see you without your clothes, Amy. I want to take you into my bed and show you what it's all about. And that," he said gruffly, bending, "is why I've tried so damned hard not to do this...."

His mouth melted into hers, soft and then hard, teasing, then rough and hungry. She went on tiptoe to link her arms around his neck. Her mouth answered the wildness of his. And she wasn't even shocked when his hands slid down to her thighs and lifted her hard against his, so that she could experience the very tangible evidence of his need.

He lifted his mouth to look at her. "You aren't fighting," he whispered.

"No, I'm not," she whispered back, and she smiled lazily, dreamily.

His hands slid up to the base of her spine and moved her gently against him. "Not shocked?" he whispered.

"No." Her fascinated hands unbuttoned his shirt slowly and then eased under the fabric to touch thick hair over bare, warm skin. Against her body, his rippled and surged.

"I'm sorry," she said, stilling her hands.

He breathed slowly, as if he were fighting to retain control. His hands cupped hers, caressing them. "It's all right," he said. His mouth touched her forehead, as lightly as a breeze. They were standing close, touching, and she made no move away from him. He smiled against her eyebrow. "I can't remember the last time I was this aroused."

She lifted her chin so that she could see his eyes. They were very dark, almost black. "Does it hurt you?" she asked softly.

"A little. No, don't move away," he protested when she started to shift her feet. "Just stand still, and everything will be fine, eventually," he added with black humor.

Her fingers reached up to the dimple in his chin. Since he didn't seem to mind that, they wandered farther afield. She explored his wide, sexy mouth, his big, straight nose, his broad forehead and thick eyebrows, to the ridge of his jutting brow, over his closed eyelids to thick short lashes.

"I like your face," she said. "It's very strong, very definite."

"Not handsome," he murmured.

"No. But sexy," she whispered, smiling.

His eyes opened, and there was something like tenderness in them. They smiled at her. "So are you."

She let her eyes drop to the massive chest under her hands, and stared unashamedly at the ripple of muscle, the mat of hair that arrowed down to the belt at his narrow waist.

"Have you ever decided?" he asked.

"Decided what?" she asked blankly, glancing up.

He chuckled. "Whether or not you like hairy men?"

"If you want the absolute truth," she confessed, "I've never been this close to a man who had his shirt off."

"What about that would-be fiancé?"

"He wore an undershirt," she told him, laughing because it was funny now, "and I never even saw him in bathing trunks. He's as thin as a rail. I suppose he's self-conscious, and I never even realized it." She studied the set of Worth's head, his broad shoulders, with intent interest. "But I've never in my life seen anyone like you, not even in magazines."

His jaw tautened, and the control he'd regained was rapidly going again. His fingers tilted her chin. "You're setting matches in gasoline," he murmured. "Watch out."

She drew in an aching breath, her eyes going helplessly to his mouth. "Wouldn't you like to seduce me?" she asked. "I'm twenty-eight, you know. A dinosaur that's outlived its time. I'll die someday, and I'll never have known what it was to be a woman."

His hands moved to her waist and pressed there so hard that she looked up. His face was rigid, his eyes sparkling with some dark emotion.

"It would complicate things too much," he said after a minute. "Grandmother needs you. If I let that happen, she could lose you. I meant it, Amy, about commitment. I don't want it. And you would."

Swallowing down her pride and the faint hurt the words inflicted, she managed a smile. "Are you that good in bed?" she whispered wickedly.

His fingers caressed her waist. "I'm experienced," he corrected. "Sex is like eating potato chips," he added quietly. "It's damned hard to stop, once you start. We'd get addicted to each other. I'm not ready for addictions."

"You're forty," she reminded him, her voice quiet, soft.

"So I'll die an old maid," he shrugged, and a corner of his mouth curved. "Amy," he added, serious now, "there was a woman. I won't go into details, but

I took a pretty damned hard blow. I'm still raw about it.''

"I understand," she said. She knew it all, but she wasn't letting on. She stared at her hands, so pale against the deep tan of his chest. "Your grandmother says that she's spent her life being careful, and now she's going to pull out all the stops and really start living. Aren't you going the other way?"

"Look who's lecturing me on involvement," he burst out laughing.

She shrugged, smiling at her own folly. "Well, yes. But, you're a man. You can go hunting. I can't. I mean, I could. But it isn't me. And I'm never going to start any fires with the male sex. I'm just not built for an endless parade of one-night stands. I don't really believe in purely physical relationships. I want a best friend as well as a lover."

He touched her cheek. "Well, you can be my best friend anytime, country girl," he said, and smiled down at her. "And my lover, if you like."

She stretched up against him with a faint sigh. "I'd like to make love with you, Worth. But you're right, it would complicate things."

"All the same," he whispered, bending to her mouth, "I like an occasional taste of you."

He kissed her slowly, wrapping her up in his big arms like a treasure, smiling against her mouth when she bit at him.

"Put your tongue in my mouth," he whispered, "and I'll show you how to French kiss."

Tingling with the sensuality of the remark, she obeyed him. And caught fire when he taught her the subtleties of open mouth kissing. When he finished, and lifted his head, she was flushed and trembling all over.

"Yes," he breathed, staring at her, "that's how you'd look at me as I took you..."

"Worth," she moaned, reaching up.

"No," he said in a soft tone. He drew her against him and held her, rocked her, close and warm until the trembling stopped, until both of them could breathe normally again.

Her eyes closed, and she felt tired, but safe and cosseted. Her cheek moved softly against his chest, and she smiled.

"I like hairy men," she whispered.

"I like women with big, sexy blue eyes. All too much, I'm afraid." He moved away, tugging affectionately at a lock of her long hair. "Come on. Show me what you want to plant. Then we'll go and have lunch with Grandmother."

"Okay."

She daydreamed about spring flowers all the way back to the house, sharing her colorful dreams with Worth, who strolled along beside her like a benevolent giant. She adored him, she thought dizzily, on fire with wanting him, caring for him. Instinctively, she slid her hand into his. He held it warmly, locking their fingers together. And she thought she'd never been so happy in all her life. What a wonderful day!

They went into the house, and just as Worth started toward the living room, Baxter came scurrying down the hall with a white face.

"Mr. Worth," he breathed quickly, "it's your grandmother. Sir, I think it's a heart attack!"

Seven

The next few hours went by in a blur. Amelia had run into the house behind Worth, to find Mrs. Carson in terrible pain, crying from the sheer intensity of it and holding her chest. Worth called an ambulance and the family doctor. Mrs. Carson was breathing jerkily, she was pale, her skin icy to the touch, and her eyes seemed sunken in her thin face. And Amelia, who'd seen enough heart attacks to recognize the symptoms, was almost certain that her employer was in for a rough time. She sat by the bedside, holding the icy hand, murmuring soft words, while Worth paced and paced, watching for the emergency unit to arrive.

Finally the ambulance pulled up, flashing red lights and siren blaring. A few minutes later, it sped away again, heading for the hospital. Worth rode in the ambulance, and Amelia drove her battered Ford along after it. When she reached the hospital several minutes later, she found Worth in the emergency waiting room. Several other people were sitting around with worried looks. Amelia edged between Worth and a fat lady with a screaming baby, and took his big hand in hers. His other hand was holding a smoking cigarette, the first time she'd seen him with one.

"Have you heard anything?" she asked softly.

"No." He stared blankly at the wall, absently lifting the cigarette to his lips.

She leaned her head against his shoulder, drained. She'd been in life-and-death situations at the hospital where she'd worked, of course, but the patients had always been strangers. This was something very different. She cared about Mrs. Carson.

She glanced up at Worth's rigid, unsmiling face and wanted to cry for him. He looked as if his world was ending, and there was nothing she could say or do to help him. He was lost in a private purgatory, hanging between hope and despair.

"I'm very sorry," she said, her voice quiet. "I wish I could help."

His fingers contracted. "Don't let go, Amy," he said simply.

She closed her eyes and held his hand, and the minutes dragged and dragged, with people coming and going, voices raising and lowering, children crying and then laughing. It was a long time before a white-uniformed doctor came to find Worth.

The big man went off with him, a few yards away. The doctor talked and Worth listened, looking more grim by the minute. The doctor shook his hand, nodded and walked back down the hall.

Worth didn't move for a minute. He stood smoking his cigarette as if he wasn't sure what to do. He glanced at Amelia, indicated that she should stay where she was, and went off down the hall.

When he came back, he looked worse than ever.

"Do you have a car?" he asked blankly.

"Yes. Mine. It's just outside."

He followed her out the door, and she hesitated about asking him anything, at least until they got away from the hospital and that terrible black look left his face.

He got in beside her, hardly noticing where he was, and lit another cigarette as she struggled to crank the old car. Finally she was able to pull it out of the parking lot.

"He doesn't think it's a heart attack," he said minutes later. "He's more inclined to believe it's angina. But he isn't volunteering anything past that, and he won't commit himself until he runs a battery of tests, including an angiogram in the morning, if she's stabilized."

"Oh," Amelia murmured. She knew what that meant, but she wasn't telling him. An angiogram, not the simplest of diagnostic tests, would tell them if there was a blockage or a faulty valve in the elderly lady's heart. And a positive reading on either of those possibilities could mean open heart surgery. Poor Mrs. Carson!

"They took her straight to the cardiac intensive care unit." He ran a hand through his ruffled black hair. "That means three visiting periods a day, about ten minutes each. I want to go back, but I need to change clothes and get my own car."

"Is there anything I can do?" she asked.

"Yes. You can stay at the house and protect me from the world for the next two days. I can't cope with business and grandmother at the same time."

"I'll go to my apartment and pack a bag," she agreed without protest. "If you'll leave me a list of people who might call, and what I'm to tell them, I'll handle the rest." She turned a corner, the car clanking at the effort, and Worth suddenly seemed to realize where he was.

"My God, it runs," he exclaimed, looking around at patched upholstery and peeling paint and listening to the ticking roar of the engine.

She was glad of the distraction. It might take his mind off the worry. She glanced at him. "Shhhh!" she said quickly. "If you insult it, it stops dead in traffic."

"How can you insult something that looks like this thing?" he asked, his dark eyes incredulous. "I had no idea it was in such terrible condition or I'd have bought you something better!"

"You aren't buying me anything, Mr. Carson," she informed him. "I can support myself, thanks."

"On tuna fish sandwiches and a car that's half wrecked," he nodded.

"I like this car. It has character."

"What it has," he returned as she pulled into his driveway, "is a warped frame, a sticky valve, a shot transmission. And how much do you have to pump the brakes to get them to work?" he demanded.

She flushed, and his eyes narrowed.

"You'll drive the Mercedes if you have to go anywhere," he said shortly. "I'll take the Rolls to the hospital."

"Worth..."

"Don't argue with me, sweet," he said quietly, and the endearment from a man who never used endearments kept her mum.

She parked the car in the garage and cut off the engine, cringing when it sputtered and knocked and pinged to a halt.

He got out, opened her door and fished in his pocket for a set of keys. He put them in her hand and closed her fingers around them. They were still warm from contact with this body.

"Don't argue," he repeated, searching her eyes. "It's insured to the hilt. If you put a dent in the fender, I won't even scowl, all right?"

"I'll be terrified," she said with a sigh.

"It's just like yours, only smaller."

"Smaller, and wildly expensive."

"Inverted snob," he murmured, and managed a weary smile for her. He bent and brushed a kiss across her lips. "Come on. I'll make a list of names for you."

He threw an arm around her and kept it there all the way to the house.

It took several minutes for him to acquaint her with the possible callers. He had business interests everywhere, including a project in South America that was waiting for a signature and would demand his presence for several weeks once the papers were signed.

"But what about your condo on the north side," she asked.

"I do have executives," he reminded her. "The secret to success if having capable underlings and knowing when and how far to delegate. I'll manage. Anyway," he added on a sigh, "it's not an immediate problem. Grandmother is." He checked his watch. "I'll need to get there within the hour, or I won't make the third visiting period. Got everything you need from me?" he asked as she went through the neatly scribbled list.

"Yes, I think so," she agreed. "I'll only be away for a few minutes," she promised. "Just long enough to get what I need from my apartment."

He nodded and started toward his room down the hall.

"Worth," she called.

He turned, big and sad and looking as if he had a ton weight on him. "Yes?"

"She's tough as old combat boots," she said. "She even told me so. If I were a gambling woman, I'd bet on her."

"So would I. But she's seventy-five, Amy."

"My grandfather," she told him, "is eighty-three and plows his own garden."

He smiled. "I like you, Amy Glenn," he said, before he turned and went back down the hall.

She was intimidated by the Mercedes, but she managed not to scratch it as she drove back to her apartment. She stopped by to tell the Kennedys what was happening and that she'd be away for a few days. They told her not to worry, they'd look after her things, and then offered any help she needed. She almost cried at the unexpected kindness. But, then, they were kind people. She thanked them and quickly drove back to the big, lonely house.

Baxter let her in, his face drawn with worry. He'd been with the family twenty years, Mrs. Carson had told her, and his silver-haired elegance went with the crystal chandelier.

"Has there been any word yet from the hospital?" Amelia asked him the minute she was inside.

"No, Miss."

She slumped a little. "I'd hoped..."

"Yes, Miss, so had the rest of us," he murmured. "She's such an indomitable person."

"A very, very unique lady," she agreed. "Mr. Carson says it's an excellent hospital, very modern. And

they can do so much for heart problems these days,"
she added hopefully.

"It's all that fried food she loves," Baxter grumbled. "Cook will humor her, and she coaxes her. It
isn't good for a weak heart."

"Aha," she said, wide-eyed. She smiled. "When
she comes home, I'll tell on her. Mr. Carson will take
care of that!"

He actually smiled, then quickly caught himself.
"Miss, if you hear anything after I've gone home..."

"I'll be glad to call you, Baxter," she replied. "I
know I haven't known her as long as most of the staff,
but I care about her, too."

He nodded and went back to his duties. Amelia
went down the hall and then stopped dead. Which
room was a guest room? She knew which was Mrs.
Carson's. She bypassed it and opened the next door.

She peeked in. King-size bed, immaculate green
patterned bedspread, green drapes and cream carpet.
She knew without glancing at the discarded clothing
in the big armchair by the bed that this was Worth's
room. She closed the door quickly and went along to
the next room. It was done in pinks and creams, very
pretty and obviously a guest room. She went in and
put her small overnight bag on the bed. It looked odd
there, so battered and worn against that luxurious
spread. She took it off and put it on the carpet. Then
she went back to the den and sat down at Worth's big
desk to wait.

He didn't call, but several other people did. Most of them were on the list. But there was a woman, a Mrs. Cade, who wasn't on the list, and she seemed to know him very well. Amelia fielded the questions that were shot at her as best she could, while she withered inside with jealousy. Worth, she thought achingly. Oh, Worth.

"I'd like him to call me as soon as he comes in," Mrs. Cade said firmly. "I am sorry about his grandmother, but this is urgent."

What in the world did she think a heart attack was? Her Scotch-Irish temper got the best of her, and she said so.

There was a stunned silence on the other end of the line. "No one speaks to me like that," came the stilted reply.

"I just did," Amelia said shortly. "And if you want Worth, you can wait until he has time to call you. Maybe you've never had anybody you love in a life-or-death situation, but he's pretty torn up right now, and the last thing he needs is to be hounded by some insensitive woman!"

"You insolent little...Who are you?" the voice demanded.

"I'm the tooth fairy," Amelia replied sweetly. "Do remember me if you shed any fangs." And she put down the receiver, hard.

He'd kill her, she thought miserably. But that horrible woman shouldn't have been so rude and unfeeling.

There were several other calls. She did the best she could, and finally, about nine o'clock, the phone stopped ringing. Thirty minutes later, Worth came in.

"Well?" she asked, rising from the desk, stiff from so much sitting.

He glanced at her, rubbing a weary hand around the back of his neck. He looked worn. His face needed shaving, and there were new lines around his dark eyes, his tight mouth. His shirt sleeves were rolled up, and he was carrying his light jacket over one arm. He tossed it into a chair and stretched.

"She's awake and cussing like a sailor," he said dryly. "They've given her something for pain. In the morning, after they've run the angiogram, Dr. Simpson can tell me more." He sighed and sat down beside his jacket in the chair. "Amy, he thinks it may be a blockage. Or several of them. He mentioned the possibility of bypass surgery. Her enzymes are normal. He says that means it wasn't a heart attack. But she's short of breath and she has an arrhythmia. If it's what he suspects, it will get worse, and eventually she will have a heart attack. She's been having weak spells, but she didn't want to worry me, so she didn't say anything." He laughed mirthlessly.

"I know about bypass surgery," Amelia said, searching his tired face. "It has a very small risk factor, and most patients are back at home only a week later."

"So he told me," he returned. "But it's going to be a damned long few days."

"I'll keep you going," she said, and smiled. "Can I get you something to eat?"

"I don't think I can eat, Amy."

"Some coffee, then? Or a stiff bourbon?"

"The bourbon, and then coffee," he said. He went to the desk and thumbed through the notes. He scowled and glanced at Amelia warily. "How long ago did she call?"

"Mrs. Cade, you mean?" She felt uneasy and averted her eyes. "About an hour or so," she said.

He stared at her. "What did she want?"

She shifted from one foot to the other. "She didn't say," she said coolly. "She only said it was urgent."

He got up while she poured his bourbon into a glass and handed it to him.

"Thanks," he said absently. He was still staring at the piece of paper.

"She's very rude," Amelia blurted out, avoiding his eyes. "And I was rude, too. If she's a friend of yours, I'm sorry."

"She was a little more than a friend, several months ago." He turned away. "I'll return these calls now. Good night, Amy."

She knew exactly what that meant. Thanks, kid, but get out of my way, I'm busy. He didn't have to say it, his attitude did.

"Baxter asked if you'd call him, too, and tell him how Mrs. Carson is," she said as she went toward the door.

"Baxter can damned well wait," he said curtly. He sat down behind the desk and picked up the receiver. He didn't even look up as he dialed the Cade woman's number.

Amelia felt sick all over. She closed the door gently behind her.

Well, now she knew who Mrs. Cade was, she told herself. Obviously, that was one of his women.

She felt empty and cold. She went to the guest room and put on her simple white cotton nightgown and took down her long hair. Well, it looked as if she was very soon going to be out of a job. If Mrs. Carson had to have that bypass, she'd need a nurse, and she wouldn't be in the market for a companion. And while Worth had tolerated Amelia, and teased her, and even made a small pass at her, it wouldn't cost him any sleep if she left. He'd told her often enough that he never wanted to commit himself again. Where, where, did that mysterious woman belong in his life? Was that the kind of woman he liked, insensitive and uncaring and aggressive? Apparently his ex-fiancée had been such a type as well. She laughed bitterly. How sad that she herself was such a wilting wallflower. Perhaps if she hadn't been a repressed virgin, she could have rushed out in her gown to seduce him. Hmmm.

Seduce him. She thought about that for all of one wild minute, and then quickly dismissed it from her mind. What a time to be thinking of such a thing, when his grandmother was desperately ill. Poor old

Jeanette. She liked her employer very much. She was going to miss the feisty old lady.

Minutes later, she was sitting in front of the vanity mirror, brushing her long hair, when the door suddenly opened and Worth stepped into the room. He looked worried. His jacket was back on and there was a dark, grim look in his eyes. For a few seconds, she didn't think he even realized that she was dressed for bed.

"I have to go out," he said abruptly. "Will you listen for the phone, and take any messages? I've called the hospital already to give the number where I can be reached."

Her pale blue eyes searched over his face like loving hands. His face was hard and drawn and his own eyes looked bloodshot. He was worried enough about his grandmother, why did that awful woman have to come along now to upset him even more? Amelia knew that was where he was going, he didn't even have to tell her.

"I'll listen for it," she promised coolly.

He seemed to notice then what she was wearing; she could see the sudden spark of interest in those haunted eyes. He smiled slowly, noticing the thinness of the white gown and the subtle contours of her body so nicely revealed by the lamplight shining through the sheer fabric. With her long, dark hair like a silky curtain around her shoulders and down her back, she had the look of a fairy.

"Well, Miss Glenn," he murmured thoughtfully, "I expected that you'd wear pajamas."

"Actually, I prefer sleeping in briefs and nothing else," she said sweetly, "but that's when I'm at home."

"Don't mind me," he mused. "I'd hate to interrupt your routine."

"I told you before, Mr. Carson, I don't do private performances," she reminded him. She put the brush down. "Was there anything else?"

"Yes. But I don't have time," he said with a wicked glance at her body and then at the bed.

"Stop that," she said stiffly.

"Why?" he asked.

Her eyes followed him. He seemed to find that disturbing, because his own narrowed, quietly assessing. And all at once, he pushed the door shut and moved toward her.

"No," she whispered. She got to her feet. That made it worse, because the gown was cut low in front, and the curves of her breasts were sharply revealed.

But he kept coming, stopping when he was practically against her. His big, warm hands rested on her shoulders, caressing, while his eyes feasted on her.

She could feel her heart going wild, her body reacting to that closeness. She adored him. The masculine scent and feel and warmth of him was getting to her.

"You have to go out," she reminded him breathlessly.

"I know." He touched her hair, sliding his fingers through it in a silence that throbbed like a heartbeat. Or was it her own heart, audible?

"Worth," she breathed, and looked up at him.

His hands framed her face. He searched her eyes, finding quiet anguish there, but not understanding it.

His dark eyes closed. He rested his forehead against hers. "Don't be afraid of me, Amy," he said quietly. "I don't want anything. I just want a little reassurance, okay? Something to help me make it through the next few hours." His nose nuzzled hers. His big hands moved down to her waist, lightly caressing. Then suddenly and swiftly, his long fingers spread, until the tips of them were just under her breasts. Until she could feel the teasing pressure, and her body began to tremble, because she wanted to know how it would feel, if he put his hands there, and she could feel their warmth and expertness.

"Then why...why don't you go to her?" she asked bitterly, hating the way her body reacted to him.

He straightened. His head lifted, studying her face. "Well, well," he murmured dryly. "Is that where you think I'm going, Amy, to work off my worry and frustration in some woman's bed?"

"Aren't you?" she asked stiffly.

"Wouldn't that be like sitting on a clam bed and sending out for baked clams?" he asked.

Her eyes sparked at him. "I'm a repressed virgin, remember? I don't even know how!"

He laughed softly, as if her jealousy delighted him. "Amelia Glenn, you delight me beyond bearing sometimes," he murmured. "Mrs. Cade, for your information, is no longer a lover. She is now the executive vice-president of one of my subcontractors."

Her face froze, and she echoed, "Executive...?"

"Vice-president," he repeated. He looked down at her taut breasts, the dark, hardened tips outlined under the too-thin fabric. "And the urgent business has to do with that South American venture of mine. She's the contact person for the project; she's been making all the overtures to the government. She just got in, and I'm going over to discuss with her, and her husband," he added emphatically, "how to proceed."

She bit her lower lip. "Oh."

"Are you cold?" he asked suddenly.

"No," she said absently. "Why?"

"Then you must be damned aroused, Amy," he murmured wickedly, and brushed a long forefinger over a hard nipple.

She gasped and started to move away.

"This won't get you pregnant," he promised, sliding a hand behind her shoulders to hold her there. "Look, darling," he whispered, coaxing her eyes down to the gown.

His slender, elegant hand unfastened the ribbons that held the bodice together, one by one, and slowly peeled it away from her full, high breasts, baring their cream and rose beauty to his eyes.

Her breath caught and she started to lift her hand to pull the gown together again, but he brought her hand to his lips and settled it against his hard, warm chest.

"Just stand still," he murmured softly. He eased the gown down to her waist while she trembled at the newness of a man's eyes on her body, and then he moved away and looked until she blushed.

"If I didn't have to see Terie," he said softly, "I'd carry you to the bed and strip you, and I'd let you feel my mouth on every inch of your body."

Her lips trembled. Her body trembled. She was being burned by a fever she'd never experienced in her life, at the mercy of unfamiliar hungers. "H...here, too?" she whispered, and brushed her fingers against her breast.

"Especially, there," he said. He caught her waist and lifted her up, so that her breasts were within a breath of his mouth. His lips parted and he brought her close, swallowing one taut, trembling nipple in the moist warmth of his mouth, savoring it.

She arched backward, her hands holding his thick, dark hair, holding his mouth over her, and she moaned.

His breath quickened, as if the sound aroused him. Blind, deaf and dumb, she felt him lift her, carry her, toss her onto the bed. And she suddenly felt cold and alone.

Her eyes opened, to find him standing over her with dark, unreadable eyes in a face like stone as he looked down at her partial nudity.

"That," he said quietly, "is highly addictive and leads to a kind of exercise you haven't experienced yet. I'm not in the market for a sensual virgin, Amy, although I'm flattered by the offer."

With tremendous dignity, she sat up and replaced her bodice, trying not to let him see the tears that were welling in her eyes.

She even smiled, although she didn't look at him. "Oh, well, you can't blame a girl for trying," she said lightly. "We old maids have to get our experience where we can."

"You're no old maid. You're a beautiful, compassionate, sexy woman. And I want you like hell. But not tonight."

"No, you have work to do," she said for him.

He started to say something, scowled blackly, and turned away. "Yes. I have work to do. Listen for the phone, please."

He went out without looking back and slammed the door behind him.

She lay awake until the early hours of the morning, when she finally heard him come back. Well, maybe he'd worn himself out enough to sleep, she thought drowsily. She only hoped the angiogram wouldn't show any need for Mrs. Carson to have open heart surgery. Since his grandmother was the only person Worth loved, it would be horrible for him.

Amelia would have to stay with him, for the time being. He might not want her body enough to risk commitment, but he did need someone, and who else was there? As odd as it sounded, she was probably closer to him than anyone except his grandmother. They'd talked a lot over the weeks and she felt that she understood him. She could give him comfort, she thought bitterly, if nothing else. She could give him that, even if he didn't want her to love him.

The next morning, she went with him to the hospital. The angiogram was run, and much later that afternoon, the doctor told Worth that his grandmother's need for a bypass was imperative, and urgent. The surgery was scheduled for early the next morning.

Worth went in to see his grandmother and came out looking wild and restless. Amelia tried to get him to eat something, but he wouldn't. She went back home finally to tell the staff what was happening and answer the mail.

She hadn't gone in to see Jeanette, because Worth was reluctant to let her. He seemed to feel that it might be upsetting for the older woman. Amelia didn't agree, but she wouldn't have argued with him for the world. Any kind of major surgery had its risk factor, and she knew even if Worth didn't that the seventy-two hours following that surgery were very precarious. The elderly woman could die. He had to know that, though, and was hoarding these last few visits with her. Amelia didn't want to deprive him of a single minute. So she sent her love instead, and then tried to keep busy at the house answering the phone and wondering how she was going to survive when she had to leave Worth.

It was late when Worth came back from the hospital, and the staff had long since gone home. Amelia had waited up, taking time to fix a platter of cold cuts and ready the coffeepot just in case he wanted food. She walked out into the hall to ask if he'd like anything. But he didn't even see her. He went straight into the den, and closed the door.

She kept thinking that eventually he'd come out. She made coffee and put some sandwiches on a platter, and then tried to think what to do. She remembered the long days before her grandmother had died, the anguish of waiting, the nearness of death and the hopelessness of being able to do nothing. It must be worse for a man, she thought. Much worse.

She paced the kitchen, her blue eyes troubled, her jeans and T-shirt confining. She was tired and wanted her bed, but she couldn't possibly just go to sleep and leave Worth alone.

Risking his anger, she put a cup of coffee on the tray with the sandwiches, knocked at his door and boldly walked in.

He was sitting on the sofa, an open bottle of whiskey and an empty glass on the coffee table in front of him. His head had been in his hands until she walked in. He glared at her, as if the whole situation was her fault, with stormy dark eyes in a face laid bare by grief and worry.

"What the hell do you want?" he demanded.

"I came to feed you, and please stop growling at me," she returned, not at all put off by his cold temper. She knew what was causing it; she could see through the anger to the pain.

"Well, I'm not hungry," he returned. He poured another glass of whiskey. "Go away."

She put the sandwiches down on the coffee table and sat beside him. He was wearing suit slacks with a totally unbuttoned white shirt. His dark, hairy chest was bare and this, added to the slight growth of beard on his broad face, gave him a disreputable look.

"I said..." he began again.

"I heard you. Have a sandwich and some coffee." She picked up a full cup and saucer and began to sip her own.

"Damn you," he said with a rough laugh.

"Old maids are stubborn," she told him. "But if you humor us, we go away."

"I'm not sure I want that." He took a sandwich and bit into it. "Chicken salad. My favorite."

"I must be psychic," she murmured, but she'd watched him, and she knew his preferences in food.

"Really? These are good."

"Thank you."

He finished the sandwich and sipped coffee, staring straight ahead. "What will I do if she dies, Amy?"

"A tough old bird like you?" she scoffed, refusing to take him seriously. "You'll manage, just as she would, if the situation was reversed. But I wouldn't give up on her, if I were you," she added. "A woman who takes up break dancing at the age of seventy-five is not really likely to let an operation get her down.''

He turned and looked at her for a long time, frowning. ''You're always like this,'' he said quietly. ''Always optimistic, encouraging. You're unique, Amy.'' He sipped some more coffee. ''I've never had anyone except my grandmother. I suppose, in the past year, I've more or less built my world around her.'' He looked up, his eyes narrow as they met hers. ''She talks when she trusts people. And she trusts you. She told you about Connie, didn't she?''

It was no time to lie. ''Yes,'' she confessed. ''She did.''

He studied his hands. ''She tried to tell me, and I wouldn't listen. I was so crazy about that damned woman that I wouldn't let myself believe what she was. Because of it, Grandmother had a heart attack. I've lived with the guilt ever since.'' He laughed bitterly. ''I've lived like a monk ever since, except for an occasional laspe. I haven't let anyone come close. I've been afraid to.''

''Are you going to punish yourself for the rest of your life for that one time you didn't believe her?'' she asked gently. ''She wouldn't want that, Worth.''

''It's easier said than done. I don't trust my judgment, Amy. I don't trust women.''

''I can understand that,'' she admitted. Her eyes wandered over him, loving the bigness of him, the strength, even this very rare vulnerability. If only it wasn't such a potentially tragic situation that was causing it.

"I wish I could say something that would help," she faltered. "I remember times like this. There aren't adequate words, you know."

His eyes stared blankly into his coffee. "I hate like hell to feel helpless. There's nothing I can do, nothing at all, except sit and wait."

"And you hate waiting," she murmured dryly.

"Yes, I know. But what you have to keep in mind is that she has competent doctors, and she's in excellent health, and she has a will like forged steel. That's a powerful combination."

"I keep telling myself that. But I can't be sure. Neither can they." He put the coffee cup down and took another large sip of whiskey.

"That can't be helping," she said hesitantly.

He laughed bitterly. "It's this or a woman," he murmured. He glanced at her. "And the only available one I know is taboo."

"Worth..." she began hesitantly.

He touched her mouth with a long finger. "I don't need a virgin sacrifice," he whispered.

"It wouldn't be one," she whispered back. Her eyes searched his. "I want you."

His breath drew in and went out very slowly. "Amy..."

"I know I'm not beautiful," she ground out. "I'm too thin, and my face has odd angles. But I'm twenty-eight, damn it, and I've been saving it all up for the right time and the right man." Her eyes, tearful, searched his. "I know you're not offering me commitment and happily ever after. I don't even care. Tonight you need someone very badly, and I'd like to be that someone. You could think of me as a bad tasting medicine...." she faltered with a wobbly laugh.

"Bad tasting," he scoffed. He bent and kissed her very softly. "There isn't one thing wrong with you, Amy Glenn, and I want you obsessively. But..."

"Let me give you the little comfort I can," she whispered. "I know all too well how long this night is going to be for you. I'll lie in your arms and hold you and you can have me."

His lips parted on a rough breath. "Amy, the risk," he began slowly.

"There isn't any risk," she lied, easing his conscience. She put her mouth very slowly to his, loving him, wanting him. It would never be more than this, and perhaps it was wrong. But she'd live on this all her life. And this poor, tormented man would be able to face his crisis tomorrow a little more rested and at peace than he would otherwise. "Please," she whispered at his lips.

With a hard groan, he pulled her into his arms and returned the kiss wildly, hungrily, his heart slamming against his chest, his breath ragged. Seconds later, he picked her up and carried her to his room.

She felt tingly all over as she looked at him, measuring the sheer size of him, all muscle, all man. She thought about lying with him in bed, with nothing between them, in the darkness, and her breath caught. Dark against light, hard muscle against soft skin...

He laid her gently on his bed, with the single lamp by the bed burning softly, and he sat down beside her and looked at her for a long time. His fingers slid under her jeans to brush over her flat belly and she tensed. He looked up at her frozen face. "Like it?" he asked gently. He flattened his hand, and it was so big that it almost completely covered her stomach. His fingers brushed, teased, and his eyes never left her face. "You're very soft."

"Your hand...is enormous," she whispered.

"Like my feet." He laughed softly. His eyes fell to the T-shirt. He eased it over her head and tossed it aside, staring down at her lacy bra, and his fingers slid up. "Now this," he said, teasing around the clasp, "is a man's delight. A catch he can see and doesn't have to feel for. It beats groping behind."

He lifted his eyes again to watch the reaction in her own as he gently dispensed with the clasp and then slowly, teasingly, peeled the bra away from her high, firm breasts. He looked down at them with an expression she couldn't define, watching the tips harden under his intimate gaze.

His fingers went to touch them, the backs of his hands rubbing the nipples, and her body tensed and shuddered as unexpected ripples of pleasure began to stir.

His fingers bunched around the hard tip and tested its texture. "I'm not quite sober, Amy," he murmured. "I should stop...."

"No!" she choked. Her body was aching. She felt her legs move restlessly, and wondered at her inability to control them. "Please!"

His eyes darkened, and she could see desire glazing in them. His hand moved again, to her waist. He held it there while he bent, and his mouth hovered just over her breast. "Are you going to be a noisy lover, Amy?" he whispered, laughing softly. "Let's see."

And his mouth opened, enveloping her, moist and warm. She stiffened and cried out hoarsely at the wild thrust of sensation he aroused with that tender suction. She felt his teeth and then his tongue, and finally his whole mouth as his hands stabbed in at her waist and propelled her upward to ease his path.

His mouth slid down her, nipping at her waist, her stomach. He tore the jeans and briefs out of his way, and his mouth nudged against her inner thighs while she moaned deep in her throat and began to move on the coverlet with involuntary sensual writhings.

He did things to her body that she'd only read about before. He touched her in places and ways that brought tears to her eyes. Her hands clawed into the pillow at her head and she wondered if she was going to survive it. The pleasure was building, growing, buffeting her.

Her eyes opened when he lifted his head to look at her, and she knew they were misty and dazed and tear-filled. Her full mouth felt swollen. It was parted, her neck arched, her body trembling and damp, her long hair in a glorious tangle around her head.

His eyes went over her, lingering on the restless, helpless movement of her legs.

Sitting up, he moved his hands to his opened shirt. He stripped it off, baring his broad, hair-covered chest. Slowly, sinuously, holding her fascinated gaze, he removed every stitch of his clothing and let her watch him. Her eyes went over him like hands, rapt with curiosity and appreciation of the rippling muscle and blatant, perfect masculinity of his deeply tanned chest, flat stomach, narrow hips and powerful thighs. He was exactly as she'd imagined he would be undressed, the image of a statue she'd seen and blushed at in a museum. But he wasn't a statue. He was real. And even as she watched, he eased down beside her on the coverlet and she felt the warmth of his skin.

He kissed her swollen mouth softly, tenderly, while his hands found her breasts and traced them in a silence that blazed with rough breathing and wild heartbeats. His fingers moved down to her flat stomach and explored it, eased to her thighs, savoring the silky skin. And all the while, his mouth invaded hers, doing such intimate things to it that she felt the heat all the way to her toes.

He took a long time, lightly teasing her body, touching and arousing it to such a fever pitch that she began to cry from the spiraling tension.

His mouth went down to her breasts again, to her belly, her thighs, and she began to move restlessly, helpless movements that signaled the loss of control.

And then she felt his weight, beside her, above her, felt the powerful warm muscles and abrasive hair of his chest, his flat stomach, his thighs, and she looked up into dark, stormy eyes.

"Please," she whispered, her voice breaking into a thousand pieces, her eyes wet, her hands reaching up, trembling as they caught his shoulders. "Please."

His hands slid under her head, his eyes filling hers, so close that she could see the tiny lines around them.

"Please," she whimpered, arching, blatantly aroused, aching all over with a need she'd never felt before.

"Gently, sweet," he murmured. His hand touched her thighs, positioning, stilling. He eased down very slowly, watching her face so that he'd know instantly if he was hurting her.

But it was easy. A little hesitation, a little tightening. But he had her so aroused that she never felt pain. She wanted anything, everything, pain would only augment the wildness, the savagery, of the desire she felt for him. Her eyes blazed with it, her nails bit into his shoulders, her teeth clenched.

"I want...you," she whispered hoarsely, her eyes telling him, her body begging for his. "Worth. Worth...!"

He moved down, smiling through his own desire as his body registered the ease of its passage, her hunger for him startling in its intensity. She was shuddering all over, her eyes as wild as her body, and she excited him beyond bearing. A virgin, but so passionate that he lost control as her movements intensified and overwhelmed him.

She matched him, move for move, her eyes wide, her body taut and fit, measuring itself to his, withdrawing, advancing, in a duel that made him laugh deep in his throat, that made him feel suddenly savagely male.

He caught her wrists and slammed them down beside her head, and watched her smile, too, as he set the rhythm and slowly increased it. He could see the fierce pleasure he was giving her in the thrashing of her head, the tenseness of her face, the tiny cries that tore out of her.

He'd meant to be gentle, but it was asking too much. With a sound much like a growl, he closed his eyes and lost himself in her, feeling the ripple, the sudden terrifying tension that built in waves until it suddenly snapped and the world went black around him as he arched up and his voice broke.

She was crying. He caught his breath and looked at her face, his body tense, still shuddering in the aftermath.

His body relaxed heavily on hers, and then he saw his hands gripping her wrists and was afraid that he'd hurt her. He released her, and gentle fingers turned her face back to his.

"Amy," he whispered softly.

Her eyes opened, wide and as blue as heaven.

"Did I hurt you, little one?" He frowned, touching her swollen lips gently. "I didn't mean to be so rough."

"Hurt me?" she managed breathlessly. "I...Worth," she said hesitantly, "was I...is it normal to feel it, like that, the first time?"

He felt as if the breath had been knocked out of him. "Did it happen?" he asked gently, and she averted her eyes, coloring delicately, and he laughed. "My God. The first time..."

"Maybe it's because I went so long without a man," she faltered, glancing up at him.

"Don't start thinking there's something wrong with you," he said gently. He brushed the damp hair away from her eyes, feeling lazy with pleasure as he felt her warm, soft body completely under him, silky skin against his own. "I took a long time, Amy. I made you half crazy before I took you, that's all. And you were lucky," he added dryly.

"It was only for a second," she said softly, searching his eyes. "But it was like dying, and so exquisite."

"The little death," he said. "Yes. For me, too. Sweet madness. Oblivion." He bent and kissed her softly. "Sleep with me."

"I thought I already had," she mused.

"That was loving," he whispered. "Sleep in my arms. And when I'm rested, and you're rested, we'll make love again."

Odd that he should call it that, she thought drowsily, when she was sure it was only a physical release for him, only sex. It had been everything for her. A wild kind of union, a joining of souls, a spiritual fusion. She watched him move beside her and the cover was gone, the bed rumpled. She sat up and looked at him, blatantly, watching him grin at her fascination.

"And you said you couldn't do it in the light," he reminded her with a dry smile.

"I didn't realize what we were doing," she confessed. "I never imagined it would feel like that. And you watched me...." She blushed.

"I had to," he told her. "I needed to know at the beginning if I was hurting you. I was afraid you might not tell me."

"Oh." Her eyes fell to his chest. "I've been afraid of that all my life, afraid that it would be so painful...." She laughed softly. "And I didn't even realize it was happening until it was all over."

"Yes, I noticed," he teased. "My God, I've never had anyone like you," he whispered, the smile fading as he looked at her. "I did things with you and to you that I've never done before. And you laughed, and your eyes were as wild as a storm, and when I held you down you matched me, took me as surely as I took you." His breath caught in his throat as he looked at her, let his eyes feed on her exquisite nudity. "I expected you to cringe and then grin and bear it. And instead, you devoured me, bewitched me. I don't think I'll live long enough to forget tonight."

"I'm glad," she whispered. Her eyes adored him. "Because I'll never forget it, either."

"No regrets?" he asked seriously.

She shook her head. "No regrets."

"Thank God. If I'm drunk, Amy, I don't want to be sober again." His hands caressed her, fascinated with her softness. he breathed slowly, but it wasn't helping. Already, it was happening again.

Her eyes brightened with a new knowledge, a new confidence. She eased down, shifting so that her body was over his. "Teach me how," she whispered, and put her mouth over his.

He made a rough, harsh sound in his throat and his hands reached for her hips.

The morning came suddenly and too soon, and Amy opened her eyes feeling a new stiffness, an odd new kind of discomfort. Her eyes went instantly to the pillow beside her and her lips parted. There was only a dent in the pillow, but Worth was gone. Worth. She caught her breath. Worth!

She sat up, and as the covers fell away, she saw her body, with new marks on it, unmistakable marks, and she realized instantly what had happened. She'd slept with him. Not just once, either. Her face went red and she bit her lip. Now what? Everything had changed, and as he'd said himself, there was no going back. She glanced at the clock and was shocked to find that it was already ten o'clock. The surgery would still be going on. She leaped out of bed, grabbed her discarded clothing, dragged it on and hurried to her own room, careful to scout the hall first.

She showered and dressed in a simple white shirt-waist dress and high heels, left her hair long because she didn't want to waste time putting it up and ran out the front door without stopping for coffee or even a slice of toast.

The servants would know where she'd slept. She didn't know how she was going to face them. Or Worth. Or his grandmother, if Jeanette lived. Jeanette had to live, she prayed. She had to, for Worth's sake. Did he regret what had happened? She hoped not. Whatever happened now, at least she had the memory of him. She'd cherish it, right or wrong, for the rest of her life.

Eight

Worth was alone in one of the waiting rooms in the cardiac intensive care unit. He was smoking like a furnace, and Amelia's eyes went over him like loving hands, lingering on the broad chest in an expensive mauve knit shirt and his muscular thighs in tailored tan slacks. He looked more handsome than ever, and she knew now what was under his clothing. Her face colored at the memories.

He looked up and saw her. She expected that he might smile at her, or hold out his hand. He did neither. His eyes were haunted as they looked at her, and all she saw in them was regret.

She went to him slowly, trying not to look too crushed by what she saw. She sat down beside him, tucking the skirt of her white dress close around her. Not for the world would she let him know how she'd hoped that the night before had been a beginning. Now she knew it had only been a momentary weakness, caused by too much liquor, too much worry, and by her own eager abandon. She wouldn't think about that, she told herself. It wasn't the time.

"Has there been any news?" she asked softly.

He shook his head and took another draw from the cigarette. "It's a long operation. Several hours." He glanced down at her searchingly. He started to say something and then shrugged. "I got here just in time to see Grandmother off." He smiled faintly. "She was awake and alert and anxious to get on with it. She said to tell you not to go looking for work elsewhere. She's not about to die and leave you jobless."

She laughed and then felt tears sting her eyes. That sounded like her indomitable employer. She lowered her gaze to her clasped hands.

He muttered something under his breath. "Amy, I suppose I should apologize for seducing you."

She glanced up at him and back down again. "I offered," she reminded him. "There had to be a first time, didn't there?" she asked evasively. "I'm twenty-eight, after all. It might be my first and last time, you know. I...don't feel that way with most men."

Her eyes searched his, sad eyes, because it had been only one night and she had hundreds ahead of her that wouldn't begin and end with him.

He didn't look convinced, though, and there was a dark scowl on his face.

"It's done," she said, crossing her legs. "Regrets won't help now."

His face hardened when she said that, but she was staring toward the hall and didn't see that he'd misunderstood what she said.

She had to get her mind off it. She stared at the doorway but it only reminded her why they were sitting there, and she frowned. Bypass surgery wasn't so dangerous these days, but Jeanette was old. And for a long time, it would be touch and go. She wormed her hand closer into his with a sigh. He was smoking madly, and she knew it was nerves. She hadn't expected that he could be nervous, but perhaps it was a mask, like the one she donned when she was afraid or worried. He seemed invincible, but Jeanette was his Achilles' heel. What would happen to him if she died?

Two hours passed, and finally a Red Cross volunteer came in, smiling.

"Mr. Carson?" she said as Worth stood up. "I thought you'd like to know your grandmother came through the surgery beautifully. She's off the respirator and breathing nicely on her own. They'll be moving her into the recovery room shortly. If you watch, you'll see her go by."

Worth laughed softly. "Well, well, and I was sitting here worrying myself prematurely gray."

"She'll be fine," the volunteer added, and winked.

"Thanks," he said.

"You're welcome." She breezed out and Worth sighed heavily. Amy grinned at him, tears in her eyes.

"She really is tough as old combat boots," she said on a watery laugh.

"I'm ready to believe it," he said.

Minutes later, Jeanette was wheeled past them on a stretcher, with an IV tube in her arm and a bottle of solution on a pole rolling right along beside her. She looked white as a sheet and she wasn't moving, but at least, thank God, she was alive.

The doctor was just behind her. He came in, called Worth to one side and explained what had been done and what Worth could expect. They shook hands, and Worth stretched hugely.

"He says it will be about seventy-two hours before we can be sure that everything's going okay," he told Amelia, reaching down a big hand to help her to her feet. "But the procedure went well and she's responding exactly as she should. He's cautiously optimistic."

"Now she'll take up tennis," she told him with a dry smile. "She was muttering something about it the other day, and complaining because of her age."

He burst out laughing. "My God, just don't encourage her!"

"Spoilsport," she chided. "I'll buy her a tennis racket!"

"How about something to eat?" he asked. "I think I could manage a sandwich if you could."

"Yes, of course."

But if she'd hoped they might talk, she was doomed to disappointment. He kept the subjects general. Politics, current affairs, even the South American project he was going to start on. He wouldn't let the conversation get personal. And then she knew that last night had been something he was uncomfortable about. Perhaps he was afraid she might want commitment, but she was going to show him that he was wrong. Just because she'd made a fool of herself once, she wasn't going to do it twice. She could be as indifferent about it as he was. So she smiled and talked, and her heart cracked open inside, where he couldn't see it.

Later, after Jeanette was moved from recovery into the cardiac intensive care unit, they were both allowed in to see her. She didn't say anything, and she seemed part of the tangle of machinery that filled the tiny cubicle. All around, there were other unconscious patients with nurses and doctors and orderlies breezing past, doing tests, taking vitals.

Worth took his grandmother's frail hand and stared down at her pasty face, with the breathing tube making something foreign of her mouth. "You're doing great, old girl," he murmured. "Hang on. Just hang on."

There was no response, but Amelia had a feeling that Jeanette had heard him and understood.

It was after dark before they left the hospital, when he was finally convinced that he couldn't do much in the waiting room and that he could be reached quickly if anything happened.

He let Amelia fix him a ham sandwich and then he went into his den to work.

"It will give me something to do," he said quietly. He searched her eyes. "You won't have to lock your door, if you'd been worrying about that."

Her eyes flickered as they met his. "Last night was a one-shot deal," she said curtly. "You needed something and so did I. We're even."

"As you say," he returned mockingly. "But I appreciate the gift of yourself, regardless of intent. It got me through a rough night." He took his hands out of his pockets and lit another cigarette. "Tonight, I'll stick to whiskey. It's safer."

She wanted to hit him, but under the circumstances, that would have been all too cruel. She turned. "Then I'll turn in. You'll wake me, if you hear anything?" she asked, remembering vividly the way his grandmother had looked.

"Of course. Good night, Amy."

"Good night."

Amelia got out her cotton gown and slid into it, then climbed between the covers with a long sigh. She turned out the lights, remembering how it had been the night before, the wildness of passion making her body burn. Potato chips, she thought miserably, you can't stop after eating just one. She tossed and turned for what seemed hours.

She tried counting sheep and forcing her mind to relax, but nothing worked. Glancing at the clock beside the bed, she saw that it was two in the morning. With a long sigh, she stared toward the window, where moonlight was streaming in. She wondered how Jeanette was, and if the morning would bring joy or sorrow. The big house seemed empty without its mistress. Lonely. It would be harder than this on Worth. Perhaps he was able to keep his mind on business, and would be diverted. He was right; sleeping together was a risk, and she should be grateful for his consideration. If only her body wasn't so tormented. Up until now, it had never known passion. But apparently passion was an addictive thing, because it was almost dawn when she slept.

The next morning, Worth left her at the house and went to sit in the intensive care waiting room until he could see his grandmother.

"And you'd better move back to your own place," he said over breakfast, his eyes dark and wary. "I can handle things now."

"God forbid that people might gossip," she tossed at him haughtily.

"It isn't my reputation I'm worried about," he countered. His dark eyes cut into hers. "Your generosity is going to get you into hot water one of these days. You give too much."

"That's the first time I've ever been accused of that," she laughed mirthlessly. She stirred her coffee aimlessly.

"You did mean what you told me?" he asked suddenly, his eyes speculative. "There's no chance that I might have made you pregnant?"

"Of course not," she lied smoothly. And felt sick, because the thought had already occurred to her. She'd taken no precautions and neither had he. She'd thought the risk was worth it, but now it didn't seem that way anymore. Now she felt guilty and ashamed and empty. And she didn't know how she was going to live.

"If...when Grandmother gets better, and comes home," he said then, "how would you feel about nursing her?"

"I'm not a nurse," she began hesitantly.

"I know that. But you were a nurse's aide. You could look after her. She likes you very much."

"Let me think about it, please."

"Of course." He checked his watch. "I'd better go. See you."

"I hope everything goes well," she said quietly.

"So do I," he said wearily, and all the apprehension he felt flickered instantly in his eyes and was quickly removed. He left without another word.

Amelia moved back into her apartment. But she started going to the hospital every day, to be there while Worth took care of urgent business that cropped up inevitably at his office. Within two days, Jeanette had her eyes open and was sitting up in bed. The breathing tube was removed. By the third day, she was ready to be moved into a private room on the cardiac ward.

"You are one more tough lady," Amelia said with a grin as she helped her employer sip some juice while Worth stopped in at his office.

"I told you so, didn't I?" Jeanette asked smugly. She tried to laugh, and caught her chest. A thin line was the only evidence of the surgery, because they hadn't used stitches at all. There was a wide, clear strip of tape over the incision. But the breastbone had been severed, and the doctor had told Jeanette it would be a good six weeks before it healed, possibly longer. She'd be able to go home Friday if she kept improving, but it would be weeks before she could move around very much.

"Thank God, I've got you, dear," Jeanette told Amelia fervently.

Amelia tried to smile, thinking how desperately she'd like to get away from the house and its bittersweet memories and having to see Worth every day after what had happened. But now she was trapped. How could she leave Jeanette?

"Was Worth very worried?" the elderly lady asked, her pale eyes solemn, her face still drawn and pale.

"Yes," Amelia said. "I'd thought at first that he was invincible, you know. But it crushed him, seeing you that way. He was afraid he might lose you. All of us were," she added on a smile. "Especially Baxter. We had to call him every night. Carolyn's been keeping everything spic and span, and Mrs. Reed," she added, "has been told that she is not to allow you any fatty, fried foods no matter how sweetly you plead."

Jeanette imitated a bulldog, glaring up at her secretary. "That's dirty pool!"

"That's survival," came the reply. "Doctor's orders. You want to live forever, don't you?" she added, teasing.

"Well…if I can break dance and play tennis, why not?" Jeanette murmured dryly.

"I'll buy you a racket. I promise."

"You're a good girl," Jeanette said, patting the slender hand beside her on the bed.

Amelia could have laughed at that. Yes, she'd been a good girl. What was she now? Worth's cast-off lover. He'd tired of her very quickly, she thought bitterly. After all, he didn't want any complications in his private life. The last thing he needed was a little country girl from Georgia who drove a battered old Ford. It didn't help to remember that she'd practically thrown herself at him.

She'd left the keys to the Mercedes on his desk and was driving that old car again, silently challenging him to forbid her. But he hadn't seemed to notice or care. Why should he, she thought bitterly. He'd had what he wanted from her. She'd wanted to comfort him, but he'd needed a woman, just as he'd said. And she'd mistaken what they'd shared for caring on his part. But men didn't have to care about women to make love to them. She should have remembered that. She should never have let it happen. It was all her fault.

But her soft heart had overruled her mind. The regrets were piling up on her, and with them a vague fear
of consequences. Of all the gross stupidity, not to have
taken precautions. What in the world would she do if
she were pregnant?

Her heart leaped. But it didn't always happen, she
told herself. Only during that fertile period. She remembered then, with cold horror, that that had been
her fertile period. Her eyes closed on a silent prayer.
Please, she thought, *please forgive me and don't let
my stupidity foul up so many lives.*

Her parents would never get over it if she were
pregnant. They lived in a small town, where everyone
would know, and the shame would never leave them.
If she stayed in Chicago, on the other hand, how could
she support a child when she couldn't even support
herself? She wouldn't be able to go on working for
Jeanette, not carrying Worth's child.

She bit her lip almost through. No, she told herself
firmly, there was no sense in this self-torment. Lots of
women had affairs. Lots of them didn't get pregnant.
Perhaps she was even barren; some women were. And
why worry herself over something that would probably never happen? She tossed back her hair and asked
Jeanette if she wanted a soft drink, and when the older
woman nodded, she went out to get it. Everything
would be all right, she told herself. And at least Jeanette was going to get well. That was one good thing
to come out of all the torment.

Nine

Amelia stayed with Mrs. Carson every day, almost all day. Worth came and went as his time allowed, but he was committed now to two projects, and they saw little of him during the day. He teased Jeanette and did what he could to make her comfortable. But he spoke to Amelia only when it was unavoidable, and he seemed brooding and reserved with her.

On Friday, he came to take his grandmother home, in her own Rolls, and the nurses stood and stared lovingly at its sleek lines. Jeanette, flattered by the interest, wouldn't rest until they'd all taken turns sitting in the front seat, sighing over the luxurious interior with its built-in stereo, TV, bar and phone.

Worth settled his grandmother in her room, in a hospital bed he'd rented for her recuperation. Baskets of flowers were everywhere, and Jeanette went into ecstasies examining them.

Amelia left her long enough to walk out to the porch with Worth. It was just barely autumn, warm and lazy days with a soft breeze and birdsongs. Amelia stood in the sunlight, bareheaded, thinking back a week to happier times, to companionship and soft loving at night. She didn't dare look at Worth, because he might not want to see that wistful sadness in her eyes.

He stuck a big hand in the pocket of his beige slacks, looking big and much darker in the suit and vest that emphasized his powerful build. His black hair had fallen onto his broad forehead, over dark eyes that grew darker as he stared down at Amelia, with her own dark hair loose and blowing in the wind around her shoulders. She wore a soft gray sleeveless dress and sandals.

"I'll be out of the country for a couple of months, Amy," he said, eyes narrowed as they searched her face. "I have to go down to Colombia, to oversee our project. It's too important to entrust to any of my executives."

Her heart fell. She lived for the sight of him. But it would be easier. She folded her hands. "When will you leave?"

"Monday morning. You can have your old room back. She'll need you at night, you understand."

"Yes."

He tilted her chin up, searching her sad eyes with his own. "It's still haunting you, isn't it? You with your strict upbringing and your puritan conscience. I should have sent you to bed alone that night. But I was half out of my mind with worry, and full of whiskey." He studied her closely. "Do you still hate me?"

"You didn't force me," she replied. "You were worried about Jeanette. I knew that."

"And took pity on me." He laughed coolly. "Your soft heart is going to be your undoing some day."

As if she'd martyred herself to comfort him, she thought miserably. But how could she deny it? The only way would be to admit that she was in love with him. And that would finish her employment here. He'd have to get rid of her then, if she showed signs of wanting to cling.

"It wasn't completely unselfish," she said.

He searched her eyes slowly, deeply, and his breath seemed to catch. "You can't know how much I wish..." He broke off and tore his eyes away to check his watch, avoiding looking straight at her. "I'm late again. Take care of her. I'll try to get home in time for supper."

She didn't answer him. Apparently he didn't expect her to. He got into the Mercedes and drove off.

Later, she told Jeanette she was going over to her apartment to get her clothes and went out to the garage to uncover her pitiful means of transport. And found it gone.

In its place was a little blue Japanese car, brand-new, with a big bow on top. There was a note as well.

"Amy, don't argue. Just get in and drive it. Your Ford is now a compact. I had it towed away for scrap. Consider this a thank-you, for all you've done. Worth."

She sputtered and fumed at his high-handedness, thought about rushing to rescue her faithful old car. And then realized that no amount of raving was going to bring it back. With a heavy sigh, she opened the door and slid in. The key was in the ignition. Forgetting the bow on top, she drove away.

But that night she tackled Worth the minute he came into the dining room. Mrs. Carson had been given her supper and was sleeping comfortably with a buzzer at her side to summon help if it was needed. Amelia was nibbling halfheartedly at a salad.

"That isn't eating," he grumbled, glaring at her bowl of lettuce and tomato. He tossed his jacket into a chair and sat down. Baxter peeked out and went back into the kitchen to bring the food.

"It is so. I want my car back," she said shortly.

His heavy eyebrows rose. "What for? It's about six inches thick by now. They run them through the crusher, you know."

"I will not accept expensive presents from you," she told him, her blue eyes spitting at him across the table. "I don't need to be paid for one night!"

The look on his face was indescribable. His eyelid flinched, as if the angry remark had cut him to the heart.

"I didn't mean it like that," he said curtly, staring at her intently, broodingly. "I swear to God I didn't, Amy."

She lowered her gaze to her lettuce. She felt sick. "I appreciate your good intentions," she said after a minute. "But I don't want your help, Worth."

"You could have been killed in that damned piece of junk," he shot at her. "It was twenty years old if it was a day. Any mechanic would have told you it wasn't safe to drive. You're no good to my grandmother dead!"

So that was it. It wasn't concern for her welfare, it was concern about an employee who was useful. She might have realized that in the beginning.

She smiled at her own naiveté. "Okay. I'll drive it while I work for your grandmother. But that's all," she added. "I won't accept ownership of it."

"You're so damned stubborn," he grumbled as Baxter came in with a huge steak and a side salad and baked potato, placing them neatly before him.

"Will you have coffee, sir?" Baxter asked.

"Yes, please. Have you fed Grandmother?"

Baxter beamed. "Yes, sir. She ate a good supper and went to sleep."

"She's resting very well," Amelia added. "I've checked on her, to make sure."

Baxter went to fetch the coffeepot and Amelia held out her own cup for a refill.

She and Worth finished the meal in silence. "You won't change your mind about the car?" he asked quietly.

"I will not."

"I owe you something, for all you've done," he began.

"You gave me a car," she said. "What do you usually give your one-night stands?" she asked with innocent mockery.

The reaction she got was astonishing. He slammed down his empty cup, breaking it in the process, and she jumped. He scowled at her, his face harder than flint. He got up and left the room without another word.

Baxter came in to see what the noise was, gasping when he saw the broken china. Amelia couldn't speak. Tears had made her throat sore. They spilled over as she tried to calm down, sipping coffee that burned her mouth. Baxter was too polite to ask questions, but he gave her a sympathetic glance as he carried the remnants of the expensive old china out to the kitchen. She couldn't look up. She was crying too hard.

She went straight to her room after she finished her coffee, and stayed there. Since Worth was home, he could go if his grandmother needed someone, she thought miserably. She stretched out on the coverlet and let the tears come. She cried for the tension of the past week, for a love she'd only discovered as she was losing it. She cried for her own folly and the possibility of consequences that could ruin her entire life. Most of all, she cried because she was hurt. Worth had looked at her as if he hated her.

That opinion seemed justified in the days that followed. Saturday and Sunday were an ordeal, because Worth was home all day, both days. Trying to keep his grandmother from seeing the tension was as hard as trying to avoid Worth. But Amelia managed it, just. It was for the best, she kept telling herself. Worth didn't want her anymore. She was nothing more than an embarrassment to him now, a regret that walked and talked, a visible thorn in his conscience.

When he announced early Monday morning that he was on his way to Colombia at last, Amelia could have cried with mingled regret and relief.

He said goodbye to his grandmother, and Amelia stayed glued to the chair by the elderly woman's bed, refusing to budge as he stood there in his neat cream-colored suit and glared down at her.

"I can be reached at the Sheraton in Bogota, in an emergency," he told the women. "I'll always leave word where I'm going to be."

Amelia nodded, her voice nonexistent. *Please, don't let me cry,* she prayed. *Don't let him see how much he's hurt me.* She clasped her hands on the lap of her green dress to keep them from trembling and giving her away. She forced herself to smile, when she felt like wailing.

"Have a good trip," she told him.

He searched her eyes, and there was something new in his, something quiet and faintly stunned. His bold gaze covered all of her, from toes to hair, and stopped briefly on her mouth.

"Take care of Grandmother," he told her. "And yourself," he added in a different tone.

"You, too," she said. She threw him a careless smile. "There are snakes in the jungle, two-legged as well as the usual kind. Watch yourself."

"Do look out for drug smugglers, dear," Jeanette cautioned, and her eyes were watchful. "It goes on everywhere, but especially there. Don't put yourself at risk."

"I wouldn't dare," he said, chuckling. He bent and kissed her wrinkled cheek. "Don't do this again," he instructed.

"I wouldn't dare." She threw his own words back at him. "Amelia will take good care of me, don't worry. Call us once a week or so, to let us know how you are."

"I will." His quiet, near-black eyes went to Amelia's creamy complexion and traced every line of her face. "Walk out with me, Amy."

"I'd rather say goodbye here, if you don't mind," she said with uncharacteristic hesitation. She smiled wanly.

"I do mind," he returned. "Come on."

With a helpless look at Jeanette, who was watching the byplay suspiciously, Amelia got up and passed by him into the hall. Worth said something to Jeanette and closed the door.

Amelia walked beside him to the front porch, pausing on the top step. "Well?" she asked coldly.

He had his attaché case in one hand. The other tilted her chin up to make her look at him. He seemed bigger than ever this close. She smelled the Oriental cologne he wore and felt his breath on her face. And hated him for the sensations that rippled in the body, in her mind.

"I can't leave with you hating me," he said, choosing his words. "I didn't mean to blow up at you over the damned car."

She kept her voice steady, although it wasn't easy. "It's okay. I've already forgotten."

His thumb smoothed over her chin and reached up to trace her bottom lip. "It wasn't what you said," he growled. "I don't think of you as a one-night stand. I never did. You made it sound cheap, when that's the last thing it was."

She wanted to ask why that bothered him, but she didn't. She shrugged carelessly. "No harm done. Anyway, it's all over now."

"Is it, really?" He searched her eyes. His kindled, darkened, his breath caught in his chest. "Come here and tell me goodbye properly."

He caught her waist and pulled her in to his body. He bent and started to kiss her, but her instincts for survival were sharp. She jerked away from him, frightened of what she might give away if those firm, warm lips came down on her own.

The look on his face shocked her. She saw surprise and sudden torment mingle in his eyes before he dropped his hand. He stared at her levelly, his eyes accusing, as if she'd hurt him."

"Don't," she whispered huskily, her big eyes wide and quiet.

"For God's sake, why not?" he asked shortly.

"I don't need pity," she said miserably. "And you don't have to feel guilty about what happened, either. We both know that you've had all of me you wanted. I'm just another castoff, like the car you got rid of." Her eyes lifted. "If it weren't for your grandmother, I imagine you'd have shot me out the door days ago."

He stiffened, his eyes grew cold. "You can't credit me with a single unselfish motive, can you? All right, Amy, you're entitled to your own opinion, regardless of how far off the mark it is. While I'm gone, you'll have plenty of time to think about it. Maybe absence will accomplish what I can't."

His eyes searched hers quietly, so intently that she felt her heart leap, and then he turned away. He didn't say another word. He didn't look back. He put his attaché case in the car, got in under the steering wheel and drove off. He didn't even wave. And Amelia stood on the steps and cried as she watched him leave, tears rolling down her cheeks, made silvery in the sunlight.

"Goodbye, Worth," she whispered.

She took her time about going back to Jeanette's room. But when she walked in, the elderly lady appraised her and smiled slowly.

"Now," she murmured. "Come and sit down and tell me why you're fighting with Worth."

Amelia bluffed it out. "He gave me a car. Tried to give me a car," she corrected.

Jeanette's face fell. "Oh. So that was it."

"I won't be treated like a charity case. I like you. I stay here because I care, not because I want to be pampered."

"You're independent and proud, Amy," Jeanette said gently. "And I adore you, because I'm independent and proud, too. I hate being waited on and looked after."

"I don't mind looking after you," Amelia said gently, and smiled. "So stop making me feel like a jailer. You just get well, boss lady, and I'll help you escape from the big dark jailer. Okay?"

Jeanette laughed delightedly. "Okay!" She yawned and blinked. "I'm so tired. Worth looked worse than I do, you know. Was he very upset?"

"Terribly," Amelia replied. She sat down by the bed. "He loves you very much."

"Yes, I love him, too. I'm sorry it was so hard on him. I do worry about him, Amy. What is he going to do when I die?" she asked softly. "I can't live forever. And just lately, I have trouble finding reasons to stay alive myself. There's nothing to look forward to. He'll never marry. There'll never be great-grandchildren." Her wrinkled face seemed to age with sorrow. "The end of the line. It stops with him. All my dreams, gone." Her sigh was bitter. "Oh, Amy, he'll be so alone."

Amelia bit her lower lip and looked down. "I know."

She felt the old, wrinkled hand sliding into hers. "It hurts me to think of him going on the way he is." The pale eyes lanced into hers. "Amy, do you ever think of him...as a man?"

It took all Amelia's willpower not to let that remark get to her. She faked a smile. "Once in a while," she confessed with just the right amount of interest. "He's very attractive."

"He watches you, Amy," she said unexpectedly. "All the time. I hoped you might feel something for him, because I think he feels a great deal for you."

Amelia had to fight down a blush. Yes, of course he did, he'd slept with her and he remembered how good it had been, but he wasn't interested in a lifetime of her. He just felt guilty.

"Do you think so?" she asked Jeanette, but she couldn't meet the older woman's eyes.

"Worth's spent most of his life alone," the older woman told her. She moved her silvery head on the pillow. "Even as a boy. He was never a joiner. Then, he went into the Marines and served in Vietnam. When he came home, he'd changed drastically. He drank for a year, and was frankly in danger of becoming addicted, until I persuaded him to get some counseling.

He quit, and he's never gone back, except for an occasional drink now and then. Then it was women, a different one every night. Until Connie." She tugged at the sheet. "He's never had much love. His parents died, and he knew that Jackie was my favorite. It was only after Jackie died that I turned to Worth. He's so used to secondhand love, Amy. When Connie betrayed him, I suppose it was just the last straw. He's drawn into himself this past year. He talks about growing old, but always alone. And so much of it is my fault. I've had a long time to live with my regrets."

"I'm sorry," Amy said. "For both of you."

Jeanette smiled wearily. "I have been tossing you at Worth, I confess it. But you're such a sweet person, Amy. So giving. Worth needs someone happy and sunny like you, to balance him, to keep him from growing cynical about life. If only he'd notice you."

He already had, but Amy wasn't going into that!

"Perhaps by the time he comes back from Bogota," Jeanette murmured thoughtfully, "things will have changed."

Those words turned out to be prophetic. Several weeks went by with Amy growing weaker and sicker by the day. By the sixth week, she was losing her breakfast regularly and certain that her worst fears had been realized. A test at a local health clinic gave her the proof. She was pregnant.

Ten

Even though she was expecting it, the news knocked Amelia to her knees. She'd been able to keep sharp-eyed Jeanette from seeing her problem, but now what could she do? Worth hadn't said anything personal to her since he'd left the country. If he had to speak to her on the phone, he was brief to the point of rudeness. Now he seemed to hate her, so how could she tell him that she was pregnant?

Jeanette needed Amelia, now more than ever. But she'd have to leave eventually, when she began to show. And then what? She couldn't bear even the thought of having Worth find out. She didn't want to know how he'd react to being trapped. She already had the feeling that she was an embarrassment to him—a used-up lover who was just in the way.

She was tormented by her own thoughts. She didn't know what to do. She loved Worth. Part of her was ecstatic about the baby. But a more sensible part was terrified. She thought about her inability to support a second person, all the pitfalls of single parenthood, her parents' reaction to her unwed pregnancy. What a mess. And all the fault of misguided compassion.

The only person she could have talked to was Marla Sayers, but Marla was out of town with Andy, visiting his mother. Amelia had had little contact with her friend since her job with the Carsons began. Marla had been busy when Amelia was free, and vice versa. Now Amelia wished she'd tried harder to maintain that friendship. She needed a friend now. And she remembered then, without wanting to, what Worth had said—that he'd be her best friend. And she started crying.

Her emotions were balanced on razor edge. She cried at the drop of a hat. She lost her appetite, because she was sick so much. And sometimes she tired so easily that it was really frightening. She felt that she could sleep straight through for days. The physical signs grew as well. Her breasts became swollen. Her waistline began to expand. And all the while she wondered what to do, and knew that things were going to get critical all too soon.

Worth's calls had decreased to one a week, and thank God he hadn't mentioned anything to Jeanette about coming home. But it was Jeanette who brought things to a head.

As Amelia was reading a letter to her one night, she fixed a level gaze on the young woman and asked point-blank, "Are you pregnant, Amy?"

The letter fell to the floor and Amelia stammered around for a reply. But what could she say? "Yes," she said miserably, and stared down at her feet. She was wearing a floppy blouse and an unbuttoned pair of slacks, and she felt as big as a house even though she was barely two and a half months along. Incredible to think Worth had been gone that long.

"It's been a long time," Jeanette said softly, "but I remember so well how it felt when I carried my son. It was my happiest year. But it isn't yours, is it, dear?"

Amelia shook her head. "I...don't know what to do, you see. My parents would be scandalized. They're churchgoing people. They live in a small community, and they didn't raise me to be promiscuous."

"You don't seem like a promiscuous girl to me, Amy," came the quiet reply. "It must have been just before you came to work for me. Do you love the father?"

Amelia nodded, but she couldn't lift her eyes.

"And how does he feel?"

Her lips twitched. "He doesn't know," she said huskily. "He seems to have no use for me now. It was just a one-night thing. I was crazy about him, and he needed me." Her shoulders lifted and fell. "And then just that quickly, he didn't want me any more. The classic situation. I suppose I panicked when I turned twenty-eight and I was alone and unmarried. Well, I'm still unmarried," she added, glancing up ruefully. "But I sure won't be alone much longer."

Jeanette nibbled on her lower lip. "There's no chance this man might want to marry you and acknowledge the child?"

"He would probably deny that it was his," she returned. "He hates me, and that's no lie. I'm an embarrassment to him now."

"He doesn't sound like much of a prize," the elderly woman huffed. "You're better off without him. But, Amy, what are you going to do?"

"I'm going to get another job," she said gently. "I'm sorry. But you must see that I can't stay here now."

Jeanette glared at her. "I'm not too old to have a child around."

"Of course you aren't," Amelia placated, "but Worth wouldn't like it. You know he wouldn't. He and I fight all the time lately. He resents the very fact of my presence. He always has."

"I know. I kept hoping that things might improve between you, you know," the older woman confessed. "But I could see the day he left that it had been rough sailing."

"It would get worse if he knew I was pregnant," Amelia continued. She had to keep Jeanette from telling him about the child, but without letting her know why. "I'd appreciate it if you wouldn't tell him. I...want to get away, before he comes back."

"Oh, I see," Jeanette said suddenly, her eyes kind and sad, too, and Amelia's heart stopped dead. The older woman sighed. "You think that his opinion of you would be even worse if he knew, don't you? But, my dear, he isn't such a bear, and he does realize that people are human, that they make mistakes. You might give him a chance...."

"No," Amelia said. "I couldn't bear it if he knew. Please, promise you won't tell him."

"All right. I promise, dear."

"I'll go home, for the time being," Amelia said, thinking ahead. "I won't tell my parents yet, but I'll go home and think it all out. I have to have a little time. And I'm not showing much yet. My parents stay so busy these days that they'll never notice the changes. And by the time I'm showing, I'll have a job somewhere away."

The older lady looked lost. "I'll miss you terribly, Amy. Is there any way I can help? Even financially..."

"No." Amelia got up, and impulsively bent to hug the old lady, gently, careful of her scar. "I love you, Jeanette Carson," she said with a wobbly smile. "I'll never forget you."

"Nor I you," Jeanette whispered.

Amelia went out without a backward glance, and by the end of the evening, she'd called her parents, canceled her lease at the Kennedys and booked a flight home the next morning.

It was hard to leave the house, to leave the memories behind and know that she'd never see Worth again as long as she lived. It tore the heart out of her to go. And saying goodbye to Jeanette was excruciatingly painful. Although there were plenty of servants, and Jeanette had promised to hire a nurse to stay with her at night, Amelia felt guilty about going. But now she had no choice. The worst, or best depending on her point of view, had happened. Now she had to make arrangements. It wouldn't be so horrible, anyway, she told herself. She only wondered if the child would mind the decisions she was having to make. He or she would grow up without a father, and that was a stigma she'd never expected to give a child of hers. It was ironic, when Worth was just the age to need children, and she was giving him one, that he'd never even know about it. She felt bitter sadness for them both.

Jack and Peggy Glenn were in their fifties. He was tall and thin and dark-eyed, she was short and blond and blue-eyed. They looked odd together, but there was such love in them for each other. Amelia had always envied them that devotion, and she'd hoped to find it herself. But all the years of searching hadn't produced it in her own life. She was pregnant, but not out of love. Her condition was due to a man's grief and lust, nothing more.

"It's so good to have you home," Peggy murmured as they made supper that first night. "We've missed you. Are you home for good?"

"I don't know," Amelia admitted. "I'm not sure. I just needed a little time to myself. I'm kind of between jobs."

"You haven't told us much about this last one. Your employer was an elderly woman, wasn't she?"

"Yes. A lovely lady. I miss her already."

"Then why quit?"

Amelia searched for words.

"Leave the girl alone," Jack said with a mock frown. "She's home, isn't she? That's enough." He

put an arm around her. "Stick with me, kid, I'll protect you from the Spanish Inquisition over there."

Peggy laughed and threatened him with the soup
ladle.

After that, there were no more questions. Amelia
settled into the routine, helping her father by fixing
meals while Peggy set type, doing odd jobs around the
house. In her spare time, she missed Worth like mad
and thought about the tiny baby she was carrying and
how she was going to make a life for it. She worried
about Jeanette, too. It had been such a blow to leave
her friend.

Her grandfather was shelling along the beach at the
end of her first week home, and she ambled lazily
along the sandy stretch in a huge, floppy pink-
flowered dress and sandals with her long, dark hair
flying in the wind, dreamily scanning the shimmering
sea on the horizon.

The grizzled, thin old man looked up from a conch
shell he'd just pried from the sand. "About time you
came home," he grumbled. "Thought you'd be over
to see me before this. I came to see you, after all."

"For five minutes, in between ball games on Sunday," she tossed back. "I've been busy. Somebody has
to feed Mom and Dad."

He chuckled. He wiped the conch off on his long-
tailed white shirt, and his whiskers seemed to with-
draw into his chin when he grinned at her. "Told them
yet?"

She stared at him. "Told them what?"

"About the child."

She froze in place. Those pale blue eyes of his saw too much. She wondered if he was guessing, and if not, how he knew.

"Women glow," he said easily. "Seen it too often not to recognize the signs. Your grandma and I had six, you know. Your dad would probably notice, if he and Peggy weren't so crazy about each other. They never look at you. I do."

"I always thought you were probably the only person around who really loved me, just because I was me," she teased, only halfway kidding.

He smiled at her. "You're my heart, girl. Always were. The best of 'em all. Fifteen grandkids, and you're the only one who came when Grandma was dying. Answer me, are you going to tell them?"

"I can't," she said simply. "They're like children themselves. It would kill them."

"How about the man?"

She sighed. "He hates me."

"Oh, does he, now?" he asked, glancing past her. "Ten to one he doesn't, or why would he make the trip down here?"

"Him? Trip?" She frowned, turned to follow his gaze and felt sick to her toes. There was only one man she knew who was as big as a house and had hair so black that it reflected in blue-black light. He was wearing a gray suit, and he looked only a little less threatening than a charging bull.

"You know him, I gather," Grandpa chuckled.

"I'm afraid so," Amelia said wearily.

"Good day," Grandpa called to the newcomer. "Nice weather for fishing. Care to try your luck?"

"That depends on the fish," Worth said coolly. His black eyes held subdued rage, and they cut into Amelia's flushed face.

"I'll be moving down the beach," Grandpa said with a wink at Amelia. "Yell if you need me. Lay a hand on her," he told Worth, "and I'll show you why they call us Georgians crackers."

He walked away whistling, tugging his captain's cap lower over his eyes. Amelia watched him listlessly, wishing he wouldn't go.

"Your grandfather, I presume?" Worth asked.

"My grandfather." She stared at his expensive shoes. "How's your grandmother?"

"Sickly," he said curtly, bringing her eyes up. "So you couldn't take it. The burden of an invalid was too much for you."

Her eyes dilated. "That's not why I left."

"Like hell it wasn't," he said, and his face was as lacking in compassion as the beach was lacking in gold. He put his hand into his pocket and drew out a cigarette. He lit it without once taking his accusing eyes from hers. "You almost took me in, Amy. I really believed in that charitable face you showed me. But it was all a farce. You left grandmother alone in that house, barely able to sit up, and ran the minute my back was turned."

"I didn't run," she said sharply. "I told her I was going, and why."

"She wouldn't even tell me you were gone," he said angrily. "I didn't know it until this morning, when I got back. You little cheat!" he accused. "You're just like the rest of your underhanded sex, out for anything you can get!"

"I turned down a car, didn't I?!" she shot back. He was upsetting her, and she was frightened. If she lost the baby, she'd never forgive him. "Go away, Worth, leave me alone!"

"Not on your life," he said curtly. "You're coming back with me, Miss Glenn. You can work out a month's notice, and then quit, but you're not vanishing at your convenience."

"I won't go back with you," she began.

"Like hell you won't. Suppose I go and tell your parents exactly what our relationship is?" he challenged, and took a long draw from his cigarette while the threat turned her face white.

"Why do you want me back?" she asked bitterly. "You hate me."

"My grandmother loves you," he replied, his voice cutting. "She's dying. She's giving up, all because you walked out on her. I've put in too many hours agonizing over her to give up now. You're going to come home with me and help her get her spirit back."

"I can't!" she repeated. Her eyes teared up as she stared at him, loving that hard face, loving every line in it. Her heart was breaking, and he was too blind to see why.

"All right, I'll speak with your people."

He turned. She caught his sleeve, staring up at him helplessly.

"I can't go back there," she whispered.

"Why not? Is your conscience hurting?" he taunted, his black eyes merciless and cold.

"You're the one with the conscience, aren't you?" she muttered, dropping her gaze to his chest. "I...have a job."

"That's too bad. I'll help you pack."

"She can't be backsliding because of me," she moaned.

"She is," he returned. His eyes cut into her face. "She's the only thing in this world I love. I'm not letting her go without a fight. If she needs you to stay alive, she'll have you."

"No matter what it does to me?" she asked miserably.

He averted his eyes. "What should it do to you?" he asked curtly, starting toward the house. "I don't mean a damned thing to you, but I thought she did."

"She does."

"What an odd way you have of showing it."

She didn't bother to answer him. It wouldn't do any good in his present mood, anyway. She followed after him slowly, her steps dragging. She liked to walk, but she tired so easily. By the time they reached the house, she was as pale as milk.

"Hello, darling," Peggy called from the porch. "I see you found her, Mr. Carson."

"I found her," he replied. He tossed his cigarette into the sand and ground it out. "Well?" he asked Amelia. "Do you tell them or do I?"

Amelia went up the steps to the spacious beach house, avoiding her mother's frowning gaze. "I have to go back to Chicago," she said quietly. "Mrs. Carson's getting worse."

"Oh, I'm sorry," Peggy said, glancing at Worth's hard, drawn face.

"So am I," Jack murmured dryly, hugging his daughter. "I'd just gotten used to having her home."

"I'll be back before you know it," Amelia told him and reached up to kiss his wrinkled cheek. "I'd better pack." She didn't look back. When she reached her room, the others were talking as easily as if they'd known each other for years.

Worth drove to the Savannah airport in the car he'd rented, his eyes on the road, never wavering as they wound through the fascinating old city with its delicate houses and multiple squares and huge, shady trees. Amelia loved the architecture, and in happier circumstances would have enjoyed the trip. But the man beside her wasn't the best of companions for sight-seeing, and she didn't volunteer any conversation. Now what was she going to do, she wondered miserably.

The airplane ride was going to kill her, she just knew it. She felt nausea rising in her throat as the plane started to shoot up into the clouds, and only in the nick of time did she make it to the rest room. She wiped her face with a damp paper towel and had to force herself to go back to the seat.

Worth stared at her, frowning. "Are you all right?"

"I've had a virus," she lied. "I'm not feeling well."

His jaw tautened as he studied her. "Do you have anything you can take for it?"

She did, but she didn't like using the tablets. She was afraid they might harm the baby, despite all the assurances by the doctor and the pharmacist that they wouldn't.

"I don't like taking pills," she said quietly.

"Do you like throwing up?" he returned.

She turned in the seat, and her blue eyes shot sparks at him. "I hate Yankees," she said coldly.

He held that mutinous gaze. "That isn't what you said the night before Grandmother's surgery," he said, his voice as soft and dark as velvet.

Her eyes closed. She didn't like remembering. She reached down for her purse and took one of the tablets from the folder. She had to make sure he didn't see that folder, because it stated in large letters that the pills were for nausea in the early stages of pregnancy. She took the coffee the stewardess had poured her and sipped a little of it with the pill.

"You look odd," Worth said after a minute.

"I lost my lunch," she said curtly, "how do you expect me to look? I'd walked down on the beach hoping the breeze would settle my stomach. And no sooner did I turn around than I saw you, and it started churning all over again."

He actually smiled, although it was reluctantly and just a twitch of his wide mouth. But his eyes searched over her as if he wanted to memorize how she looked.

"My God, it seems like years since I've seen you," he said under his breath.

"Does it? I'd hoped that it would be years before I saw you again," she said waspishly. "Light-years."

He sighed angrily and lit a cigarette.

"Do you mind?" she challenged. "I'm sick enough as it is!"

He hesitated, but only a second, before he ground it out. "You're making this damned difficult."

"So are you. I'm sorry about Jeanette. I love her, too. But I can't spend my life in Chicago, and especially not near you! I hate you!"

He didn't move a muscle. He seemed to stop breathing. His hand went blindly to a magazine in the pocket at the back of the seat ahead. He took it out, crossed his long legs and began to read as if he hadn't a care in the world.

She leaned back against her own seat with tears stinging her eyes. She was sick and lonely and afraid. What would she do if he realized what was wrong with her? What would she tell Jeanette? She couldn't ever remember feeling so helpless. And he didn't even care. That was what hurt the most. He didn't even care.

If she could have seen the blank, dark eyes that were staring so unseeingly at the pages of that magazine, she might have changed her mind. They held a kind of torment that would have intensified her tears.

Hours later, he was pulling his own Mercedes up at the door of the house. Beside him, Amelia was tired and almost asleep from the combination of the pills and the long journey. All she wanted was to lie down, but Worth wasn't going to allow that, she knew.

She'd been so unhappy when she said goodbye to Jeanette. Now he was going to put them both through it again. How could she leave a second time?

He got out her suitcase and closed the trunk lid. "Here," he said, tossing her overnight case toward her, "make yourself useful."

She deliberately let it fall, afraid that the strain of trying to catch it might hurt the baby. It crashed onto the steps and bottles shattered. She stared at it blankly.

"Well, my God, excuse me," he said curtly, bending to lift it. "I didn't realize you were too weak to lift a case. Open the door, then."

She did that, and she never looked at him.

"There's just one other thing," he said, pausing with her in the hall, and his eyes were threatening, cold. "Don't get any ideas about staying longer than it takes to get her on her feet again. I don't want you here. The sooner you're out of my life for good, the happier I'll be. You were a sweet diversion that night, but I've had my fill. I don't want you, in any way, now."

"That works both ways," she said in a ghostly whisper.

He led her down the hall, pausing at the door of his grandmother's room. "Go ahead. I'll put your bags in your room."

She opened the door, and Jeanette looked up from the bed. She looked ten years older, haggard, weak, pale as death.

"Oh, Jeanette," Amelia whispered tearfully. She ran to the bed, and the old lady held out her thin arms.

"Dear girl," the quavering voice whispered back. "My dear girl, I've missed you so much! Did he drag you back, is that why you're here? And how are you? The trip must have been terrible for you."

"I was sick half the way here," Amelia whispered. Her head nestled beside the silvery one on the crisp pillow cover. "But now I'm glad I came. What's happened to you?!"

"I have no appetite," Jeanette said wearily. "No will to live. I told you before you left, dear, I can't see the future anymore."

"But you must," Amelia said. She sank down on the bed beside the withered little body and held the thin hand. "Worth is home now."

"Yes, he is," came the grudging reply. "About ten minutes a day, he's home. And when he's here, he roars around like a train, and curses the servants.... I don't know what happened while he was gone, but he's changed dreadfully."

"What about the nurse you were going to hire?" Amelia chided gently.

Jeanette pursed her lips and made a rude sound. "I hate nurses." She glanced up at the younger girl. "I missed you. We had a lot of fun together."

"Yes, I missed you, too," Amelia said with a soft smile. "But I don't know how I'm going to manage being here until he thinks I've worked out enough of my time. I'm afraid he'll notice."

"You could just tell him, you know," Jeanette suggested. She sighed, as if talking was an effort. "He'd understand. It isn't completely your fault, the man has to take some of the blame. It isn't easy to get pregnant without help, you know, even Worth would realize that."

"Pregnant?"

The man in the open doorway had turned a pasty shade, his tan eclipsed. His dark eyes went homing to Amelia's body, and he stared at her while wheels clicked over in his head. Amelia could almost see them turning. Her nausea, the loose clothing, the way she'd dodged that bag he tossed her, her unwillingness to come with him on the plane. His eyes closed. His face hardened.

"Oh, sweet God," he whispered, shaken. "And I forced you to come here, putting the child at risk. What have I done?"

Eleven

Amelia stared at him with conflicting emotions. He looked devastated by what he'd learned so unexpectedly, but how did he feel about the baby? Trapped, angry, contemptuous, afraid...how? Her big blue eyes watched him closely, like a hunter trying to find a sign in a dark forest. But when his eyes opened again, they were as blank as a piece of paper. He simply looked at her, and looked and looked, as if he'd only just met her.

"I'm sorry," Amelia whispered unsteadily. "I didn't want to come back, you know. If you hadn't insisted, you'd never have found out."

His face contorted. "My God, is that why you left?"

"Of course it's why she left," Jeanette broke in, glaring at him, and her voice was stronger than it had been since Amelia walked into the room. The elderly woman dragged herself upright in her frilly pink bed-jacket and fixed a scalding eye on her grandson, who was still looking as if he'd been shot. "She knew you had a low opinion of her, Worth, she was afraid that you'd hold her in contempt if you knew. She swore me to secrecy before she left."

Amelia had to struggle for the right words. She shifted restlessly on the bed. "I've told your grand-mother that the father doesn't know," she told Worth, making it sound as if the father was some shadowy person because she didn't want to betray him. Her eyes pleaded with him to go along with the fiction, not to upset his grandmother with such a personal scandal. "I don't want him to know. It's my baby. I'll have it and raise it and love it, all by myself."

"You will not," Jeanette said haughtily. "You'll stay here and I'll help you. And if Worth doesn't like it, he can move out," she added with a sharp glance at the frozen features of her grandson. "A child around the place might keep me alive for years and years. I love children."

Worth finally jerked away from the door frame and came into the room. He stared down at Amelia with eyes so dark they seemed like black marbles. He ran a rough hand through his thick, straight hair, so that it fell roguishly onto his broad forehead. He looked so big, and Amelia knew so well the touch of his skin, the strength in those hard muscles. She dropped her eyes to the bed, so that the memories wouldn't have to torment her.

"Amazing," Worth said quietly, "that you'd try to protect me, after the way I've treated you."

He dropped down in the chair beside the bed, staring at Amelia while Jeanette glanced from one set face to the other and frowned.

He took Amelia's free hand in his, feeling its coldness. His dark eyes went to meet his grandmother's. "There's something I have to confess," he said gently. "The man she's trying so hard to protect is me. I went to her for comfort the night before your surgery, Grandmother, and out of misplaced generosity, she gave everything I asked for. The baby is mine."

Amelia looked up at him, pained. "Oh, Worth," she whispered. "I'm sorry!"

His fingers contracted around hers. "It takes two," he said, his voice deep and rough.

Jeanette's face was glowing, her lifeless eyes suddenly sparkling, a happy dancing blue as she caught her breath. "The baby is my great-grandchild?" she asked delightedly.

"I'm afraid so," Worth returned with faint humor. His dark eyes searched Amelia's shamed ones. "There isn't the remotest possibility that the baby could have been fathered by anyone else."

Amelia's lips trembled. She lowered tear-filled eyes to her lap and saw the tears splatter onto his haircovered wrist.

"Don't," he whispered. He produced a handkerchief and dried her eyes. "Don't. Everything is going to be all right now."

"Of course it is, my dear," Jeanette said gently. She reached out and stroked Amelia's long, disheveled hair. "Worth and I will take care of you. A baby," she sighed, dreamy-eyed now, so different from the defeated-looking woman she'd been only minutes before. And then it hit her. "But, my God, Worth, you aren't married!"

"We will be within the week," he said imperturbably. He got up, sticking his hands in his pockets to study Amelia. "And don't argue," he told the young woman, who'd just opened her mouth to protest. "If you do, I swear I'll call that photographer who snapped you in the trench coat out here, and I'll give him a Pulitzer-prizewinning shot! And then I'll mail a copy to your parents, Amy. I mean it. You're marrying me, whether you like it or not."

"Damn you!" Amelia fumed at him.

"So that's how you got her to come back with you," Jeanette murmured dryly as she studied her grandson. "You threatened to tell her parents what you'd done, didn't you?"

"It was the only way to get her here," he confessed on a heavy sigh. "I saw history repeating itself," he said gruffly, turning away, and Amelia and Jeanette exchanged knowing glances. He went to the window and smoothed back the curtain. "It's funny," he said, laughing bitterly. "I can do cost estimates in my head, I can beat out competitors on contracts, I can put up enormous skyscrapers. But when it comes to people, I just can't seem to read character." He turned slowly, his eyes dark with regret as they touched Amelia's face and body. "Amy, I said some horrible things to you today. I hope eventually you may be able to forgive me for them. And for what I've done to you. If it's any consolation, I'm no happier than you are about the situation."

So he didn't want the baby, she thought. Well, it was what she already knew, wasn't it? She felt old.

"Why don't you go and lie down?" Jeanette told her gently. "I'm better already. I daresay I'll eat a monstrous supper now that I have so much to antici- pate. I can knit, did you know? I'll make the most precious little booties and caps. Make her lie down, Worth," she told her grandson. "She needs lots of rest now. And send Baxter in here, I want him to go to town and get me some yarn." She frowned. "We'll need to put wedding announcements in the papers, and Amy must call her parents...."

Worth gestured Amelia out into the hall while Jea- nette was still talking and closed the door behind them.

Amelia quickly moved away from him and went to the guest room. Her eyes fell when she saw the bed, and all the memories came flooding back of the last time he'd been in here with her.

Her bags had been put on luggage racks, the only indication of occupation. She smelled perfume and knew it must be from a broken bottle in her cosmetics case.

"I'll buy you some more toiletries," Worth said as her eyes went to the square case. "I'm sorry I tossed the case to you like that. I didn't know you were preg- nant or I'd never have done it."

"Don't bother handling me with kid gloves," she said shortly. She sat down on the bed and with a long breath stretched out, dangling her feet over the side. "I'm so tired," she whispered. Her eyes closed.

"Tired and sick and upset, all of it my fault," he said quietly. He bent and took off her sandals before he pulled a quilted pink coverlet over her legs.

Unexpectedly, he sat down beside her, and her eyes flew open, wide and a little frightened.

"I won't hurt you," he said gently. His hand eased down to her tangled hair and smoothed it away from her face. "I'm sorry. About everything."

Her eyes closed so that he wouldn't see the tears. She could manage if he'd been angry, but that unexpected tenderness got to her. "I tried to keep you from finding out," she whispered brokenly.

His hand stilled. "Yes, I know." His fingers touched her lips. "Open your eyes, Amy."

She did, and found him staring at her with an expression she couldn't quite explain.

"Why didn't you want me to know about the baby?" he asked gently.

He didn't seem angry now; only curious. It calmed her a little.

"Because," she began, her fingers restlessly pleating the coverlet, "I didn't know how you'd react, or even if you'd believe it was yours."

"Are you out of your mind?" he asked. "How could it be someone else's?"

"You might have accused me of sneaking around," she muttered.

"Sure. With who, Baxter?"

Her lips made a thin line.

He smiled slowly. Accusing eyes, mutinous mouth, exquisite color in her face. He studied her mouth. "You've given Grandmother a new lease on life. Now she has something to look forward to."

"Yes, I saw that," she said. Her eyes fell to his chest. "At least somebody's happy about it."

"Aren't you?" he asked gently, and tilted her chin. He searched her eyes. "Don't you want the baby?"

"Of course I want it, but you don't!"

His heavy eyebrows went straight up. "I don't?"

"You didn't want commitment, remember?" she shot at him, dragging herself into a sitting position to glare at him. "No strings, you said, just a sweet interlude, you said!"

"And I thought you'd only pitied me, and that's why you gave yourself."

"I pitied myself, for being so stupid and—"

He bent forward and stopped her mouth by placing his against it. She started to draw away, but his hand slid behind her neck and kept her there.

"No," he whispered. "Sit still."

Her fingers went to his hand. "Worth, don't, please...."

But his mouth coaxed and teased, and before she could find the willpower to resist him, the old magic was beginning to take her over. She felt her mouth softening, opening to the warm persuasion of his. She felt his tongue teasing the inside of her lips, probing further, felt his hands suddenly reach for her and bring her into a warm, fervent embrace.

"Oh, Worth," she moaned, half protest, half pleasure. Her arms enfolded him, her mouth returned the hungry pressure of his. And the whole world seemed to spin away.

"My baby," he whispered against her lips, easing her back down on the bed. "You're carrying my baby...."

The thought seemed to inspire him to even greater efforts. She drowned in warm, hungry kisses, arched her body to hands that were gentle and slow and expert on her swollen breasts. Her eyes opened as he lifted his head, and she felt a breeze and realized that he'd opened her dress all the way down the front. He was looking at her, seeing the subtle changes that even the early days of pregnancy had made to her slender body.

"Very pretty," he whispered with a purely masculine smile, the conquering male surveying his conquest and liking the visible evidence of it. "Your breasts are bigger."

"They're swollen," she said shyly.

"This is darker." His fingers traced around the hard nipple. His eyes dropped to the slight swell of her abdomen above the pink bikini briefs she was wearing.

He hesitated before he reached down to touch it, as if he was afraid he might hurt her. He looked up into her eyes with a question in his own as his hand slowly flattened over his child.

"My God," he breathed, searching her face. "I never connected lovemaking with this," he confessed. "I never even considered that a baby might come of it."

"Men don't, do they?" she asked gently. "Did you think women got them from the garden, under leaves?"

He smiled back. "No."

His face was tender now, not accusing or cold, and she warmed to that tenderness.

"I'm sorry I left so quickly," she said. "Jeanette promised to get a nurse, and I was so frightened...."

His eyes narrowed. "I can imagine," he replied. He bent and kissed her forehead, so gently. "I'd gone off like a timber wolf to lick my wounds. I thought I could get over you, so I didn't ask to speak to you when I phoned. I'm sorry about that. You could have told me if things hadn't been so strained between us."

"To lick what wounds?" she asked hesitantly, fixing on that unexpected confession.

He lifted his head and studied his hand on her abdomen. "You wouldn't let me kiss you, before I left," he replied quietly. "You jerked away, as if I disgusted you."

Her breath caught. "Oh, no!" she said, lifting her hand to his face. She touched his cheek, feeling it go rigid. He caught it and ground his mouth into the palm. "No," she repeated, looking at his dark head as it bent. "It wasn't disgust! I thought you hated me. And I knew if I let you kiss me it would be the way it was a minute ago, I'd go to pieces, and then you'd see that it was all a front."

His eyes lifted, searching, waiting. "That what was all a front?" he asked in a deep, quiet tone.

"All that cold pride I was showing you," she said simply. "You didn't want me, and I knew it. I didn't want to embarrass you."

"I didn't want you?" He laughed faintly, as if he found that amusing. He looked down at her bareness. "I didn't want you!" His chest rose and fell roughly. "I stopped eating and sleeping. I lost a contract because I couldn't think. I went to bed with the memory of your mouth on mine, I woke up aching because I wanted to roll over and kiss you awake and you weren't there. I walked around as empty as a tomb for weeks and months, and came back hoping to make you see that you weren't a medicine I'd only taken for temporary relief. And you were gone."

"Worth, don't let me trouble your conscience too much," she said, touching his dark hair, as she felt a rush of compassion for him. He had wanted her, after all, even if love hadn't entered into it. Perhaps, in a way, he'd suffered as much as she had. "I wanted you, too," she confessed. "You didn't force me."

His fingers locked with hers and he sighed. "I thought you hated me for it, Amy," he murmured. "I hate myself, because of the way it happened."

"I was worried about Jeanette, too," she told him. "Not as much as you were, I'm sure, but I understood what you were going through. I knew you weren't thinking straight. It didn't matter. And you gave me...more pleasure than I ever expected to feel. You showed me that I wasn't too old to be a woman."

"You're more woman than I expected to find in a repressed twenty-eight-year-old virgin," he murmured dryly. He shook his head as he looked at the bare pink flesh he'd exposed. "God, what a beautiful body you have, Miss Glenn." His fingers brushed down her body to her abdomen. "Are you going to let me have it when we're married, Amy? Are you going to sleep with me?"

Exquisite thought, it made her tremble with pleasure. "If you want me," she said.

He only laughed. "Yes. I want you. I'll try to curtail my traveling as much as possible, too, so that I'll have more time to spend with you while you're carrying the baby." He took a last look at her nudity and slowly buttoned the dress up again. "That's enough of that. Get some rest, darling. I'll see you later."

Her face colored as she thought about being with him, sleeping in his arms. There were deep hurts on both sides from the past few months, but she loved him. And he wanted her. Perhaps there was some hope left.

The wedding took place a week later, at a justice of the peace's office, with Jeanette wobbly but radiant standing beside Baxter to witness the brief ceremony. Worth had seemed enthusiastic about marrying her, and Amelia was both surprised and pleased by his easy acceptance of her new status in his life. If anything, he seemed radiant. And he'd been so attentive in the past few days that even Baxter had started to grin behind his hand. One morning, Worth had brought her breakfast tray, and he hadn't been satisfied with her nibbling, so he'd fed her every bite of it himself. The tender, caring way he acted made her feel exquisitely warm and safe. If only he loved her, it would be heaven.

They'd decided not to go away for a honeymoon, because Worth didn't want Amelia on a plane again despite all her protests that she'd be fine. So Jeanette decided to spend a couple of days with a friend across town, and wouldn't be argued with. They needed some time to themselves, she informed them, so shut up. She felt fine and wanted to get out of the house.

She left early in the afternoon. Worth and Amelia had a quiet dinner together and then went to watch a movie he'd bought for the VCR.

It was a love story, something she hadn't expected that he'd like, with a wildly adventurous theme and some uproarious comedy. By the time it was over, her stomach ached from laughing.

He grinned at her. "I saw it in New York on a business trip," he told her, "and I had to have it. The heroine reminded me of you. Impulsive and adventurous and very, very lovely."

She blushed at that personal remark and smiled up at him shyly. "I'm plain, actually," she whispered.

"You're pregnant, actually," he returned, letting his dark eyes wander over her. They were sitting together in a love seat in the big living room, with the doors closed, the curtains drawn, the lights off. Except for the light from the screen and the whir as the videocassette automatically rewound, there wasn't a noise or light in the room.

His breathing became audible, over the soft sound of the recorder. He touched her throat, brushing it, teasing it. He bent and slowly put his mouth over hers. She let him kiss her, turning to him, glorying in his slow, sweet ardor.

"I want you," he whispered into her lips. "I want to have you, right now."

Her lips parted as he touched her body with hands that were softly arousing, tender. "Worth, the servants..."

"It's nine o'clock, they've all gone." He kissed her again. His breath was coming quickly, his heartbeat was audible. "Amy," he groaned as the kiss grew deeper. "Oh, God, Amy, I'm burning up," he breathed into her open mouth. His kisses were harder now, his hands urgent. "Amy, let me," he whispered, easing her down into the cushions. "Let me."

"Worth...you're so big...." she protested breathlessly as his weight settled on her, as she felt the sudden, swift pressure of his aroused body.

"I won't hurt you," he whispered. "I won't hurt our baby."

"Oh, I know that." She laughed unsteadily. "But, darling, the love seat is so short!"

"Call me that again," he murmured, nibbling her ear as his hands searched for fastenings and slowly eased her clothing away between kisses.

"Darling," she obliged. Her fingers unbuttoned the casual shirt he was wearing, and she caught her breath as his broad, hair-matted chest lay bare to her hands. She caressed him wildly, on fire with the long abstinence, with remembered passion and fulfillment. "Darling, I want you, too, I want you so much, Worth!"

"I'll give you my body," he whispered, reaching down for his belt. "All of it, here, now. It's been so long. I'm so hungry for you, Amy."

Her arms enfolded him as he moved, and she kissed him fiercely as his body found adequate space to maneuver and took slow, sweet possession of hers.

He laughed shakily, delightedly. "Oh, yes," he breathed as the rhythm built and she made a wild little noise under his mouth. "Yes! My God, you burn me...!"

She wanted to repeat that for him, but it was happening already, much too soon, much too soon. She closed her eyes and felt the exquisite tension build and build until it snapped like a spring and sent her down into the exquisite flames, and she burned up in a kaleidoscope of ecstatic color.

He was trembling. She came slowly back to awareness, feeling his heavy heartbeat, his ragged breathing, the dampness of his skin on hers, the force of his formidable weight. She caressed his shoulders and smiled into his throat.

"Worth," she murmured drowsily.

"I lost it," he whispered. "I'm sorry...."

She bit him delicately and laughed when he stiffened. "I lost it, too, so there's no need to apologize."

He lifted his head on a steadying breath and searched her drowsy, sated blue eyes. "I love doing this to you," he whispered. "I love seeing your eyes afterward. We didn't hurt the baby?" he added suddenly.

"No." She smiled as his hand touched her abdomen. Her long fingers pressed his closer. "It's only the last six weeks or so that they don't want me indulging."

"You're almost three months along, aren't you?" he asked, counting mentally.

"Almost. He'll start moving in another month and a half," she added, and laughed at his expression. "Didn't you know, Worth? They kick. At first it will be tiny flutters, but eventually we'll be able to feel little hands and feet.... Worth!"

His eyes had misted. He made a rough sound and buried his face in her throat. She held him, shocked.

"That's the Italian in my ancestry coming out," he murmured, not at all embarrassed. He nibbled at her neck. "It's an emotional thing, fathering a child. And to think about tiny hands and feet!" He took a deep breath. "My God."

"You really do want the baby, don't you?" she asked gently.

"I want him, all right." His face nuzzled hers. "I'll love him like mad, Amy."

"Yes. So will I." Her eyes closed as she drew him down hard against her. "He'll be someone of my very own to love and to love me. My parents care, but they love each other so much, there's hardly enough left for another person."

"I saw that," he whispered. He kissed her ear, her cheek, her temple, her eyes. "All I've ever had was Grandmother. And until Jackie died, I was second best even then." He sighed. "There was a woman who said she loved me and only wanted what I had. I've got a lousy track record with love, too, Amy."

Her hands touched his dark, cool hair. "Worth...I..." She swallowed and searched for the words while his big, warm body went curiously still.

"Would you mind very much if...well...if I...someday...fell in love...with you?"

His breath started again, in spurts, his hand slid under her neck and began to massage the nape absently. "Do you think you could?" he whispered hesitantly. "I've been cruel to you, Amy."

"Only because I hurt you, and didn't realize that I had." She kissed his throat, his chin. "Oh, Worth," she whispered, pressing wild, sweet little kisses all over his face. "Worth, if you'd let me love you, I think I could give up breathing!"

An odd sound tore out of his throat. His mouth slid across her cheek to find her own, and he kissed her into a sobbing, trembling submission with lips that were hungry and possessive and urgently demanding. His body trembled, and she felt a wetness on her face that she wasn't sure had come only from her own eyes.

"Let you," he ground out, and he sounded hoarse. "Oh, God, don't you know what I feel for you? Can't you see it, hear it, feel it?" He lifted his head and stared down into her eyes with a wild hunger that a blind woman couldn't have missed. "Amy, I love you, too! I love you so much!"

Her arms drew him down to her; her eyes bled tears as she kissed him, savoring him, adoring him with her mouth and her hands and her body. It was a dream come true. It was the world and the sun and moon, it was breath itself.

"Now make love to me," she whispered brokenly, nibbling at his mouth. "Now, take me, and we won't hold back anything, anything at all, darling."

He framed her face in his hands and his lips moved against hers. "Yes," he whispered. He made her part of him, he watched her as he rocked against her, seeing the love, feeling it. He smiled shakenly and bent to her mouth, trembling all over. "And so we truly love," he whispered as it began all over again.

It was midnight before he carried her into the bedroom, leaving discarded clothing all over the living room and the VCR still purring away.

"Everybody will know," she murmured drowsily.

"They're all human," he reminded her. "And all married, too. Let them snicker. I'm a bridegroom, what the hell do I care? I'm not supposed to have any sense on my wedding night."

"If you did have any, I've deprived you of it," she teased gently, her eyes loving as they met his. "Worth, if Jeanette had kept improving, would you still have come after me?"

"Of course," he said. "She wasn't all that ill, you know," he added with a smile as he closed the door behind them. "She was lonely. And so was I. I couldn't live without my heart, so I went to Georgia to find it again and bring it home." He drew her closer. "I won't ever let it go, now."

She reached up and kissed him. "I'm very glad. And the baby? You really don't mind."

He laid her down on the bed, standing over her magnificent in his nudity, faintly amused. "Well, let me show you how I feel about the baby."

He opened his closet door. Teddy bears and baseball bats and gloves and dolls and rolling toys and mechanical toys and stuffed tigers all rolled out onto the carpet in glorious profusion.

"Now," he said, hands on his hips, "do you have any more questions?"

She could only laugh. "No, darling. Not a single one."

She held out her arms and he went into them, and the eyes of one of the teddy bears reflected the lamp. The bear seemed to be laughing as the light switch went off and plunged the room into a warm, secret darkness, full of love and new promise.

The Silhouette Cameo Tote Bag Now available for just $6.99

Handsomely designed in blue and bright pink, its stylish good looks make the Cameo Tote Bag an attractive accessory. The Cameo Tote Bag is big and roomy (13" square), with reinforced handles and a snap-shut top. You can buy the Cameo Tote Bag for $6.99, plus $1.50 for postage and handling.

Send your name and address with check or money order for $6.99 (plus $1.50 postage and handling), a total of $8.49 to:

Silhouette Books
120 Brighton Road
P.O. Box 5084
Clifton, NJ 07015-5084
ATTN: Tote Bag

SIL—T—1

The Silhouette Cameo Tote Bag can be purchased pre-paid only. No charges will be accepted. Please allow 4 to 6 weeks for delivery.

Arizona and N.Y. State Residents Please Add Sales Tax

Offer not available in Canada.

You won't want to miss a single one of the heartfelt stories presented by Silhouette Special Edition; and when you take advantage of this special offer, you won't have to.

You'll also receive a FREE subscription to the Silhouette Books Newsletter as long as you remain a member. Each lively issue is filled with news on upcoming titles, interviews with your favorite authors, even their favorite recipes.

To become a home subscriber and receive your first 4 books FREE, fill out and mail the coupon today!

Silhouette Special Edition®

Silhouette Books, 120 Brighten Rd., P.O. Box 5084, Clifton, NJ 07015-5084

Silhouette Desire

COMING NEXT MONTH

CAUTIOUS LOVER—Stephanie James
Jess Winter was a cautious lover, but Elly Trent knew there was warmth locked beneath his controlled facade. Perhaps playing the seductress would provide the key. . . .

WHEN SNOW MEETS FIRE—Christine Flynn
Life in the frozen beauty of the Aleutian islands was exactly what Dr. Tory Richards needed, until things started to heat up when steel-eyed Nick Spencer literally crashed into her world.

HEAVEN ON EARTH—Sandra Kleinschmit
When Samantha met Jason she felt as if she had stepped into a romance novel. But when she learned that he was actually her favorite romance author, fact became stranger than fiction.

NO MAN'S KISSES—Nora Powers
Hilary had always tried to avoid Justin Porter, but now a debt forced her to work on his ranch. Could she prevent herself from falling under his spell again?

THE SHADOW BETWEEN—Diana Stuart
The sale of the McLeod mansion drew Alida Drury and Justin McLeod together in the game of intrigue and romance that strangely echoed the past and cast shadows on the future.

NOTHING VENTURED—Suzanne Simms
Wisconsin librarian Mary Beth Williams took a gamble and headed for Las Vegas in search of excitement. She found it when she met Nick Durand and hit the jackpot of romance.

AVAILABLE NOW:

A MUCH NEEDED HOLIDAY
Joan Hohl

MOONLIGHT SERENADE
Laurel Evans

HERO AT LARGE
Aimée Martel

TEACHER'S PET
Ariel Berk

HOOK, LINE AND SINKER
Elaine Camp

LOVE BY PROXY
Diana Palmer